"*Running away again, Tessa?*"

An old hurt pierced Max's heart.

She looked angry enough to slap him. "I don't know *what* I'm doing. All I know is I've tried my darnedest to be what you and Ryan need—"

Max pushed the hurt away. "And you've done a terrific job." He hadn't expected to say that, but he realized he'd never meant anything more.

Tessa seemed stunned. "You're just saying that to make me feel better."

"I'm saying that because it's true." He leaned forward with the word *friendship* focused in his mind—right before his lips met hers. He kept the kiss quiet, controlled, but the singeing heat of their lips meeting surged through his blood like liquid flame.

When he leaned away, Tessa pulled in a breath and expelled a sigh.

"Friends?" he asked, reminding himself again.

She looked confused for a moment, then nodded.

And at that moment Max knew he was lying to himself.

Dear Reader,

This month we have a wonderful lineup of books for you—romantic reading that's sure to take the chill out of these cool winter nights.

What happens when two precocious kids advertise for a new father—and a new husband—for their mom? The answer to that question and *much* more can be found in the delightful *Help Wanted: Daddy* by Carolyn Monroe. This next book in our FABULOUS FATHERS series is filled with love, laughter and larger-than-life hero Boone Shelton—a truly irresistible candidate for fatherhood.

We're also very pleased to present Diana Palmer's latest Romance, *King's Ransom.* A spirited heroine and a royal hero marry first and find love later in this exciting and passionate story. We know you won't want to miss it.

Don't forget to visit that charming midwestern town, Duncan, Oklahoma, in *A Wife Worth Waiting For,* the conclusion to Arlene James's THIS SIDE OF HEAVEN trilogy. Bolton Charles, who has appeared in earlier titles, finally meets his match in Clarice Revere. But can Bolton convince her that he's unlike the domineering men in her past?

Rounding out the list, Joan Smith's *Poor Little Rich Girl* is a breezy, romantic treat. And Kari Sutherland makes a welcome return with *Heartfire, Homefire.* We are also proud to present the debut of a brand-new author in Romance, Charlotte Moore with *Not the Marrying Kind.* When the notorious Beth Haggerty returns to her hometown, she succeeds in stirring up just as much gossip as always—and just as much longing in the heart of Deputy Sheriff Raymond Hawk.

In the months ahead, there are more wonderful romances coming your way by authors such as Annette Broadrick, Elizabeth August, Marie Ferrarella, Carla Cassidy and many more. Please write to us with your comments and suggestions. We take your opinions to heart.

Happy reading,

Anne Canadeo
Senior Editor

HEARTFIRE, HOMEFIRE
Kari Sutherland

Silhouette
ROMANCE™
Published by Silhouette Books
America's Publisher of Contemporary Romance

To Liz, Janie and Anne. My Leslies.

To Janet, my friend in the search.

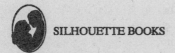 SILHOUETTE BOOKS

ISBN 0-373-08973-2

HEARTFIRE, HOMEFIRE

Printed in U.S.A.

Books by Kari Sutherland

Silhouette Romance
Heartfire, Homefire #973

Silhouette Special Edition
Wish on the Moon #741

KARI SUTHERLAND

is a former English teacher and home decorator, who likes to mix and match colors as well as words. She says redecorating a room is almost as satisfying as writing a book. Almost. She has read romances since she was a teenager. When back surgery interrupted her life-style, writing romances rather than reading them became her escape, work and emotional outlet. She resides in Hanover, Pennsylvania, with her husband of twenty-two years and their twenty-one-year-old son. Kari loves kittens, romantic movies that make her cry and peaceful surroundings.

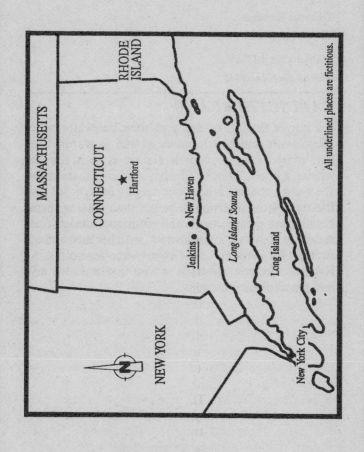

MASSACHUSETTS

CONNECTICUT

★ Hartford

RHODE ISLAND

Jenkins • • New Haven

Long Island Sound

Long Island

NEW YORK

New York City

All underlined places are fictitious.

Prologue

The May breeze wafting through the kitchen window ruffled Tessa's brown curls as she stared at Max Winthrop's broad back. He peered out the back door, watching his son play on the swing set in the yard. His shoulders, usually so straight and strong, slumped slightly in his red and white polo shirt.

Tessa didn't know whether to go to Max or not. Long ago she'd blocked out the memories of the summer they'd spent together before she'd taken off for New York, before he'd gotten to know Leslie. All these years Tessa had relegated him to being her best friend's husband.

Now Leslie was gone. The past two months Tessa had been in Jenkins, Max had isolated himself. After Leslie's death, Tessa had tried to offer Leslie's family comfort, tried to help Max with Ryan as much as he'd let her. But he was a proud man, insisting on handling his responsibilities himself. She wished he didn't disapprove of her life-style so. She wished he could accept her help.

Crossing to the door, she stood beside him. "Max?"

He stared straight ahead. "Ryan's only four. What's he going to do without her? What am I going to do without her?"

Tessa couldn't keep from reaching out to him. She couldn't keep from laying her hand gently on his arm. "You're strong, and Ryan's resilient. You'll get through this. You'll go on with your lives."

Max turned to her then, his whiskey brown eyes moist. "I miss her."

His sadness released Tessa's, and her throat tightened. She and Leslie had depended on each other; they'd been as close as two friends could be. "I do, too."

Tessa didn't know how it happened, but suddenly Max's arms surrounded her and she held him tight. As her hands rested on the warm skin of his neck, as she felt his heart beating under hers, as she felt his strength and comfort, she unexpectedly felt something else, too. She tried to push it away. It came back.

Max needed her comfort so she didn't pull away. But she held perfectly still and didn't breathe in his male scent, she shut out the sound of his heart, she blocked out the wonderful feel of muscled arms surrounding her. And she told herself she was just lonely, grieving, missing the one person in the world she'd felt closest to. This moment would never happen again.

She had to get back to work. The assignment waiting for her in Italy would help her heal. Traveling around the world had made her a person who belonged everywhere rather than someone who belonged nowhere.

Max would heal, too. All he needed was time.

Chapter One

Three years later

Tessa stood at the bottom of the ladder, looking up. "Max?"

A shingle came sliding down the garage roof and landed on bushy stalks of white pincushion mums. Max's voice carried over the edge with it. "Tessa! I thought you were arriving next week."

"I finished my assignment and decided I could use some R and R now."

"I'll be down in a minute."

Tessa never waited if she could help it. Her sneakers made no sound as she climbed the ladder tilted against the detached garage. Her jeans rubbed the rungs; her oversized navy-and-red striped shirt blew away from her back and puffed behind her as she reached the top rung.

When Max saw her, he shook his head and gave her a wry smile. "I thought I told you I'd be down."

No one had answered the front door to Max's Cape Cod. On an Indian summer Saturday afternoon, she'd known Max and Ryan wouldn't be cooped up inside. "I wanted to see the view. Look at the orange, red and yellow trees against the blue sky. Don't you wish you could take a picture in your mind and keep it forever?" She started to climb the slight incline to reach the peak where he stood.

Max gave her one of his penetrating looks. "You might be used to mountains, but I don't want you falling from my roof."

He was referring to her trip covering the latest team who'd climbed Mount Everest. "Max, you worry too much."

She couldn't keep from staring at his bronze shoulders gleaming with sweat in the late-afternoon sun. Since the day when she and Max had comforted each other, Tessa had kept her distance from Max, though not from Ryan. She loved her godson, and as she had every September since he'd been born, she'd come back to Jenkins, Connecticut, for his birthday.

Suddenly a zooming ball of motion sped into the yard. "Tessa! Tessa!" Ryan shouted as he saw her travel bag and laptop computer on the ground and her on the roof. "You're here! My birthday's not till *next* Saturday. Hey, Dad, did you know she was coming today?"

At the sound of Ryan's voice, Tessa spun around and her foot slipped. Before she could take a breath, Max caught her around the waist. Suddenly she smelled hot sun, hot male, and she knew if she turned her head, her nose would brush the soft black curls on Max's chest. The roof whirled, colors blurred, and she put her hands on his arms to hold herself steady.

"Will you get off the roof now?" he asked in a low, controlled tone.

She didn't think it was the roof that was making her shaky. "All right." She called to Ryan. "I'll be down in a minute."

Max took his arm from around her waist. "Let me go down first so I can hold the ladder."

She smiled and teased to cover the disturbing sensations that lingered. "I'll let your macho tendencies dictate...this time."

He returned a slow, reluctant smile. "But I'll pay for it in the future?"

"You bet."

Max climbed over the top rung of the ladder. Tessa always demanded notice. It was her verve, her energy, her intensity. Yes, he'd been attracted to her once... before she'd left him for a career. Before he'd become involved with Leslie. He'd always been thankful Leslie had visited Tessa that summer in the Poconos, thankful for his marriage, thankful for the wonderful result—Ryan.

Tessa didn't wait until Max was on the ground before she started down the ladder, and he shook his head with exasperation. She was almost in front of him, almost between his arms, before he could move away. He felt the backs of her thighs against his chest and momentarily lost the urge to step aside.

She paused to look at him over her shoulder. "I'm okay now."

Startled by his unexpected reaction to her, Max moved to the left and held the ladder with one hand.

Seven-year-old Ryan wrapped his arms around Tessa's legs and squeezed so hard she almost lost her balance. Smiling, she squeezed him back. "Hi there, pancake. I've missed you. What have you been up to?"

"I was nex' door playing with Scruffy. Emma says she can't throw the ball as good as she used to. You *are* gonna stay 'til my birthday, aren't you?"

His next-door neighbor was in her sixties and owned a mutt Ryan loved to play with. But Max forgot about Emma and her dog to listen to Tessa's answer to his son's question.

"I sure am. Let's go into the house and call a motel so I don't have to camp in your backyard tonight."

"Aw, Dad, can't she stay here? It'll be great. Like a sleep-over. Since I can't go with her like I used to and stay at Nana's house anymore..."

Max thought of Leslie's parents—the only caring family Tessa had ever experienced. Five months ago they'd moved to Arizona to find relief for Ryan's grandfather's arthritis. They'd hated leaving their grandson, but he and Ryan were supposed to visit them next summer. Max wondered if they could also somehow manage a visit to his parents' farm in Nebraska. It was important for Ryan to stay in touch with his extended family.

"I don't want to put your dad out," Tessa said softly.

"But we can't make pancakes in the morning if you're at a motel," Ryan wailed.

"We could go out for breakfast instead," she offered.

"Dad..."

Max met Tessa's gaze. She'd never stayed in his house before. But it would be stupid for her to rent a motel room. She'd been Leslie's best friend. Why shouldn't she stay? He went to the ladder and shifted it sideways to prop it against the garage. "You're welcome to stay here, Tessa."

She glanced at the pile of shingles on the ground and for the first time in her life sounded...cautious. "I don't want to get in Mrs. Clark's way."

"I let her go at the beginning of the summer. I'm not coaching basketball this year, so we decided to try it on our own."

Tessa's eyes widened. "But you love coaching."

"I felt Ryan and I needed time together, and coaching was taking up too much of it."

Tessa studied him for a long moment, then nodded, as if she understood. "Then if you're sure you don't mind, I'll stay."

Ryan jumped up and down and cheered. But after one look at Tessa's small, tilted-up nose, her wide green eyes and her wind-tousled hair, Max wondered if he'd just made a monumental mistake. Tessa could be a handful. Then again, he could handle anything for a few days.

Max grabbed his shirt from the branch of a bush, shrugged into it and swept up Tessa's bag and computer before she could protest—which she usually did. She was the most independent woman he'd ever met. He supposed her background had something to do with that. He didn't know much, just that she'd spent part of her childhood in foster homes.

Once in the house, he put her computer on the desk and was about to carry her bag upstairs when Tessa noticed the blinking light on his answering machine. "Are you expecting a call? I gave my service your number until I checked in at a motel."

Max said to Ryan, "Go on up and get washed up for supper."

"Pizza?" Ryan asked hopefully.

"If that's okay with Tessa."

"Pizza's fine," she agreed with a smile, knowing Ryan would eat pizza every night of the week if Max would let him.

Max hiked up the suitcase. "I'll put this in the guest room. Go ahead and listen to the message. It's probably for you, anyway. Call me if it's not."

She pushed the Play button and heard, "Mr. Winthrop, this is Mrs. Barrett, Ryan's teacher. Please give me a call." She gave the number where she could be reached.

Tessa called up the staircase. After Max came down, he replayed the tape and then, with a deep frown, picked up the phone. "I wonder what's wrong?"

Hearing only Max's side of the conversation, Tessa watched the staircase so she could occupy Ryan if he came down. After a brief interchange, Max replaced the receiver, looking worried. "Mrs. Barrett wants to meet with me Monday after school. Ryan's having some problems, and she wants to intervene as soon as she can so they don't get worse."

"What kind of problems?"

"She mentioned inattention, reading difficulties, problems making friends."

"My Lord. In the first few weeks of school?"

"She's good, Tessa. She's been with the district about ten years. She wouldn't have called on a whim; she has too many other concerns."

Max taught math at the high school, rather than in the elementary school where Ryan attended, but Tessa supposed teachers' professional reputations were no secret. Especially in a town as small as Jenkins. "Did Ryan have any problems last year?"

"Not that I'm aware of."

At Max's grim expression, Tessa felt compelled to offer, "I'll go with you if you'd like." She didn't know how he'd feel about it but was surprised by how much she wanted to help if he'd let her. Was that because nothing she could do had helped Leslie? Nothing had kept the cancer from taking her away.

"I don't want to disturb your schedule."

"I'm working on a few articles, but there's no reason I can't take some time out to help Ryan. Maybe I'll hear something you don't. I know how meetings can be."

Max looked at her for a long, probing moment. "All right. If you want to come, it can't hurt. I know you love Ryan." Max paused. "He has seemed quieter lately and he's been spending more time in his room. I've tried to get him to talk to me...."

Trying to ignore the fact that Max's shirt was still open down the front and the tails weren't tucked into his jeans, she touched his arm. "Don't borrow trouble, Max. Where does she want us to meet her?"

Max looked at her hand on his arm. "In her classroom at four."

Tessa pulled away as a chill ran up her spine, and she suddenly realized what she'd offered to do. Meeting with Mrs. Barrett wasn't a problem. Meeting in a school building was. She hadn't been thinking. If she had...

She wouldn't rescind her offer, though. So she'd be uncomfortable for a little while. Ryan mattered. She had to do this for him and to give Max support. She'd deal with her own demons afterward.

A few hours later, Tessa joined Max to say goodnight to Ryan. She sat at the foot of the bed while Max read to his son. Horses, cats and puppies danced across the curtains and bedspread. Ryan was growing and changing. She'd seen that just in the last few hours they'd played board games. She'd visited Jenkins last spring before Leslie's parents had moved. Ryan had grown at least an inch since then. But he'd also changed in some interior way. She couldn't put her finger on it, except he was more subdued.

Max closed the book and laid it on the nightstand. Ryan reached up and wound his arms around Max's neck. "G'night, Dad."

Max leaned away and brushed his son's hair across his brow. "Night."

The scene almost brought tears to Tessa's eyes. Max's love was so evident, his sense of responsibility so complete.

As Max rose from the bed and moved toward the doorway, she went to the head of the bed, gave Ryan a hug and kissed his cheek. "Sweet dreams. I'll see you in the morning."

"Hey, Dad, do we have blueberries and everything else Tessa needs?"

"Sure do."

Whenever she visited, she made blueberry pancakes for Ryan. It was one of the few things she cooked on a regular basis. He always ate at least three; that's why she'd given him the nickname "pancake." She gave him a grin and a thumbs-up sign and followed Max down the stairs.

"Another piece of pizza?" Max asked with a nod toward the kitchen.

"Sounds good. Pizza's rare where I've been lately."

While Max heated a few pieces in the microwave, he stared out the window into the dark yard.

Tessa guessed he was thinking about the meeting with Ryan's teacher. "It won't do much good to worry."

He turned around and crossed his arms over his chest. "That's what parents do. And when there's only one parent—"

"You do a good job, Max."

"Apparently not good enough." The beeper went off on the microwave. He transferred the dish to the table.

Nothing she could say could change his mind right now. She poured two cups of coffee and took them to the table. "What do you have planned for tomorrow?"

"Ryan and I sometimes go to the roller-skating rink on Sunday afternoons."

"That sounds like fun." She sat and took a bite out of her pizza. The cheese strung out and fell down her chin.

Max caught it with his thumb. The pad of his finger slipped along her skin. Tingles chased each other up her neck, and nine long years seemed to fall away.

Max leaned back against his chair and wiped his thumb on his napkin, as if he'd just wiped Ryan's chin. "You haven't gone skating for a while?"

Apparently he did *not* feel the same sensations she did when they touched. He was probably still in love with Leslie. And shouldn't he be? "Ah, college. Leslie and I went with a group from the dorm."

"It's hard for me to imagine you two as roommates, let alone best friends. You were so different."

They certainly were. Leslie was silk and lace and perfume. Tessa was jeans and cotton and fresh air, if she had anything to say about it. Max's comparison unsettled her, although she'd often made it herself.

Finishing her pizza quickly, Tessa dumped her coffee into the sink and rinsed the mug. "I'm going to head up to bed or Ryan won't get his pancakes until afternoon."

Max tossed the napkins into the trash. "We have to make the bed. I don't have sheets under the spread."

She smiled. "To cut down on housekeeping?"

He shrugged. "Mrs. Clark stripped it before she left. I never bothered to remake it. I guess I hadn't thought ahead to your arrival."

"It seems funny to be staying here," Tessa mused, wondering if that's what was making the difference in her awareness of Max.

He nodded but didn't say how he felt about it. But that wasn't unusual. Max rarely expressed how he felt except where Ryan was concerned.

Max pulled the sheets from the linen closet in the hall while Tessa went to the spare room. Peach-flowered curtains spilled around the windows and matched the spread Tessa tugged from the bed. Leslie had loved to decorate, to mix and match colors. But she was a flower person. Almost all the drapes and upholstery in the house had flower designs of some kind. Tessa liked swirls and patterns and bolder colors.

The dresser was the same dark pine as the four-poster. When Max came into the room, the space seemed to get smaller. Tessa looked at him, really looking at the man he'd become for the first time in years.

When she'd first met him, she'd seen him as a good-looking, former basketball player who knew what he wanted from life—a teaching position, a home, a wife, children, and a stability Tessa couldn't begin to fathom. Now she saw a strong man whose strength came from the depth of his convictions, decency and caring—a man who loved his son and still believed in traditional values.

Tessa knew she was strong, too. She'd had to be, being shuffled from one foster home to another. But tradition didn't mean much to her. How could it when she never seemed to fit in to her surroundings?

Max shook out the sheet and flipped it over the expanse of the mattress. Tessa caught the edge and her gaze met his across the bed. Was he remembering the summer they'd spent together? The walks? The kisses that had made her wonder what she was giving up when she left him? And she had left him. If it had been *his* choice . . .

Tessa lowered her gaze and tucked in a corner. When she stooped, the ring on a chain around her neck swung free of her neckline.

Max came to the foot of the bed. "Is that from someone special?"

She automatically reached for the circle of gold and protectively covered it with her thumb. "Not in the way you mean." Realizing she was being silly, she slowly took her hand from the ring, letting it dangle.

Max stepped closer until he was in front of her, until she could see the worn buttonholes on his flannel shirt. He lifted the small antique-looking band set with opals. "In what way? I don't remember ever seeing this before."

"It was my mother's. I wear it when I travel, when I'm away."

His brows hiked up. "I never thought you were the sentimental type."

The only explanation she had was, "It's all I have that was hers. She put it on my thumb the morning she left."

His gaze filled with compassion. "You never told me that. I guess I thought you were abandoned as a baby. How old were you?"

His compassion unnerved her, and she wanted to run. "Six. If I'd been abandoned as a baby, I might have been adopted." The loneliness was there for him to hear. She'd thought she'd discarded it along with her knee-high socks.

He seemed to hesitate for a moment before asking, "Did you look for your mother?"

"As soon as I got my first job in New York and could hire a PI." Tessa remembered her disappointment, her hurt, her anger when the man had given her the information she'd sought. "She'd died from pneumonia five years before in a women's shelter. I guess she never managed to pick herself up."

"I'm sorry. It must have been a shock."

"It was. I guess I always hoped some day I'd find her and have a mother...some sense of permanency. But it wasn't to be. At least I know she was never in a position to take care of me, so she *couldn't* get me back even if she'd wanted to."

"I'm sure she wanted to."

Tessa had wondered about that all of her life and hoped it were true.

"So why do you do it?"

Max's question seemed out of context. "What?"

"Keep hopping from one place to another. You call London your home base, but you're only there a few weeks at a time, if that long. You've had so much moving around in your life. Why don't you put down roots?"

She could tell him she didn't know how to belong. She could tell him she was afraid to keep still because so many people had abandoned her, including Leslie. But she didn't. She'd decided long ago not to feel sorry for herself, to take control of her own life and make it what she wanted it to be.

"When I was a kid, Max, I didn't have choices. My mother made one for me, so did the human services department each time they didn't know what to do with me. When I graduated from high school, I decided I'd go where *I* wanted to go, be where *I* wanted to be."

He said gruffly, "You made that clear to me when you left for New York after our summer together."

He'd never brought it up before. Neither had she. They'd both gone on with their lives. Max had gotten to know Leslie and had loved her as deeply as a man could love a woman; Tessa was sure of it. With Max, Leslie had found her vocation and career, being a wife and mother. And Tessa...

Tessa had known herself well enough to know she'd needed freedom of choice, freedom of space, freedom to grow, all on her own terms because she'd been trapped by the system for so long. She'd never resented Leslie's marriage to Max.

But now being here with Max, in his house, had stirred up feelings she'd thought were gone. In some ways, her life was no different now than it had been nine years ago. She still needed her work; it was the major force in her life. As far as relationships were concerned, her one try in the midst of a foreign war had failed badly. So that left her where she'd always been. On her own.

Lifting the ring, she dropped it back inside her blouse.

Max watched the soft material mold to her breasts as it settled into place.

Stooping to tuck the sheet along the side of the bed, she realized nothing had changed. As he returned to his side of the bed, she knew he understood that, too.

Tessa worked in the kitchen Monday afternoon, humming along to the radio on the counter. She didn't dislike cooking; she simply didn't have much experience doing it. She usually ate on the run, tossed a salad, picked up something wherever she happened to be. But there was no reason she couldn't throw together a dinner so Max didn't have to worry about it.

Max. When he stepped too close, when they laughed together as they had yesterday at the roller rink, she'd felt young, gauche, unnerved. But it didn't matter. She'd be gone in a week. Tessa put the roast in the oven and wrapped potatoes in tinfoil. She was making a salad when the phone rang.

"Hello?" an elderly woman asked.

"Yes, this is Max Winthrop's residence. Tessa speaking. Can I help you?"

The older woman's voice trembled. "This is Emma Duffrey. Next door. Max always says if I need anything..."

Tessa knew Max's neighbor. She'd spoken to her now and then on her visits. She'd seen Emma yesterday evening walking her little dog Scruffy and had chatted for a short while.

"Sure, Emma. How can I help you?"

"I fell and hurt my arm. Thank goodness I made my pies for the church bake sale this morning. I can't get hold of my daughter. If you could just take me to the emergency room in New Haven..."

"I'll be right over." Tessa checked her watch. She could make it to New Haven and back and still be on time for her appointment with Max. She was sure of it.

Chapter Eleven

Chapter Two

Tessa pushed her hair from her eyes as she parked in
the school lot. Thank goodness she hadn't gotten
caught in traffic. She was about twenty minutes late.
The emergency room had been busy, and Emma hadn't
yet been X-rayed, but her daughter had finally arrived.

Running up the steps to the school, Tessa pulled open
the glass door and felt like a child again. A few paces
into the hall and she shivered. After-school silence was
unnatural. The halls seemed to echo with muffled children's voices.

The school corridors were shadowy. Despite artwork
hanging on bulletin boards splashed with fall colors, she
remembered not laughter and academic successes, but
taunts of children dressed better than she and stern
voices that seemed to control her destiny. She'd sat in a
hallway like this one after a day in first grade while the
principal called her mother. Or tried to call her mother.
The principal had been a man, taller than the tallest

tree, or so it had seemed to a first grader. Tessa hadn't known how to tell him she and her mother had been living in their car for a week.

The authorities had never found her mother. Tessa had never known her father. The ring was her only memento of the family she'd never known. Social workers over the years had told her her mother must have loved her very much to give her up so she could be cared for properly. Tessa had preferred to believe that. It was the only way she'd survived in the children's home and in the foster homes where the authorities had tried to place her as a teenager.

Her sneakers squeaked on the tile as she rushed to Ryan's classroom, pushing away painful memories. Max had given her directions to the room. He stood there now, in front of the door in his navy suit, his arms crossed over his chest, looking fierce enough to make her want to turn around and go back to Emma.

"Where the hell have you been?" he asked in a low voice. Before she could answer, he went on, "You knew what time we were meeting Mrs. Barrett." His gaze flicked up and down her sweatshirt and jeans, her wind-tossed hair. "Or did something more important come up?"

She would have told him why she was late, but he was condemning her without a trial. "Did you start yet?" she asked evenly.

"No. You said you wanted to be included. Mrs. Barrett has been gracious enough to wait but—"

"Then let's not keep her any longer than necessary," Tessa suggested smoothly as she slipped by Max into the classroom.

He followed but glared at her while she introduced herself to Mrs. Barrett and sat in one of the chairs provided in front of the desk. She made a point of not looking around the room, not getting involved in her surroundings.

The middle-aged teacher with the pleasant smile said to Tessa, "Mr. Winthrop tells me you're a close friend of the family."

Mrs. Barrett didn't look like any of the teachers Tessa had ever had, not with her swingy, chin-length hairdo and her bright red suit. "That's right. Is there anything I can do to help Ryan?"

"Needless to say, Mr. Winthrop has asked me that same question. He says he's tried talking with Ryan. And I've tried talking with Ryan to find out if something is troubling him."

Tessa crossed then uncrossed her legs. Out of the corner of her eye, she saw that Max was watching her restlessness with a frown. "You don't think this is a learning problem?" she asked the teacher while she willed herself to relax.

Mrs. Barrett leaned forward. "We could have him tested for learning disabilities. But sometimes his work is up to par; sometimes his attention is focused. He seems distracted more than anything else." She sighed. "This might not be complicated at all."

Tessa became involved in what Mrs. Barrett was saying and forgot about where she was. "I don't understand."

"Some children get disrupted easily. They could watch a monster cartoon, get frightened and be afraid to go to sleep every night for a year until they grow out of the fear."

Tessa certainly understood childhood fears... and nightmares.

"And you think it's something like that with Ryan?" Max asked.

"I don't know. But with Ryan losing his mother, all kinds of fears could be bothering him." She explained to Tessa, "Mr. Winthrop has talked to Ryan about his mother being in heaven, being an angel now and watching over them both. And Ryan seems to accept that. But you never know what goes on in a child's mind."

"So what can we do?" Tessa was a purpose-oriented person; she wanted something concrete to tackle.

Mrs. Barrett looked down at her notes for a moment. "We could bring the school counselor in on this, but my instinct tells me that Ryan won't be any more open to her than he is to me." She looked up. "He needs someone he already knows."

"But not me," Max said grimly.

"As teachers, Mr. Winthrop, you and I both know a parent can be too close to a situation. How often have the boys you've coached or the students you teach opened up to you?"

Max thought about it and nodded. "You're right. They tell me things they'd never tell their parents. Still, I want to be the one Ryan trusts."

"You can support him. You can be there when he needs you. Ms. Kahill, I understand you're in and out of Ryan's life like a favorite aunt."

"Yes. Some visits are longer than others."

"I don't know how much time you have to spend with Ryan right now, but maybe encouraging him to share what happens at school, what he's thinking, what he's feeling, might give us a clue as to what's going on with him."

"Of course, I'll try. I wish I could do more." She felt Max's gaze on her.

"Maybe this is my fault for not dating, for not having a woman around," Max said.

He was taking the whole burden on his shoulders. Tessa wished she could put her arms around him, give him a much-needed hug and tell him none of this was his fault. "I'd imagine it would have to be the right woman, Max."

He bristled. "I wouldn't have anyone around Ryan who wasn't 'right.'"

"I didn't mean that. I just meant you can't date to find the right person for you and expect Ryan to get along with each one."

"I certainly wouldn't be parading women in and out. You know me better than that."

He was still annoyed with her for being late, and she was making matters worse. She glanced at Mrs. Barrett. The woman was watching them speculatively, and it made Tessa uncomfortable.

"Mr. Winthrop, there's no one answer. Just listen to Ryan carefully. Let him elaborate on anything he wants to talk about."

"What about the problem he's having with not making friends?" Max asked.

Tessa nodded. "At the roller-skating rink, he wanted to stay with us instead of skating with children he knew. Is that normal?"

"He probably feels more secure with you. Encourage him to play with other children. Maybe invite some of his classmates over. If he's on home turf, he might feel more self-confident to interact."

When the conference was over, Tessa's surroundings began to close in on her. She did her best to ignore the school smells of floor wax and chalk, the sight of frosted classroom-door windows, the books stacked on a cafeteria-style table outside a classroom, as she walked down the hall trying to keep up with Max's long-legged stride. Instead, she concentrated on Ryan and his problems that could become more serious if they weren't dealt with now. Would it make a difference if she stayed in Jenkins longer than a week?

When they reached the parking lot, she stopped at Max's car instead of going to hers. "I'm sorry I was late, Max. You know I wouldn't have missed this meeting."

"Do I? For all I know you could have gotten a phone call and taken off for Timbuktu."

She took a step back. "I wouldn't do that to Ryan."

"I'm never sure how your priorities stack up."

"I love Ryan and want to help him."

Max studied her, searching. His eyes darkened, and she wondered what he was thinking.

"Don't you believe me?" she pressed.

"I believe you want to help. I don't know if you can. Commitments aren't your style."

The blow was swift, neat and unexpected. It hurt like hell. Tears threatened. Tessa turned from Max and went to her car. She heard him call her name, but she slammed the door, put her key in the ignition and backed up. Leaving the parking lot, she didn't look back.

The hurt lingered as she drove back to Max's, glad he had to pick up Ryan at the baby-sitter's, where Ryan went after school every day until Max picked him up. While she was here, he could just come straight home...if Max would let him.

The smell of the roast and baking potatoes met her at the door. The salad was half made, and the carrots, tomatoes and cucumbers were still spread across the counter. Thankful she had a few minutes alone, she washed her hands, set the table and finished the salad by the time Max and Ryan arrived.

Ryan came barreling in the door before Max. He ran to Tessa, grinning from ear to ear. "Dad asked me what I want to do for my birthday. Can we go camping?"

Tessa looked at Max. "Camping? That sounds like a great idea. If I'd known, I would have brought my tent and sleeping bag."

"You have a tent?"

She crouched down to his level. "Sometimes there aren't hotels at the places I go. Do *you* have camping gear?"

"Sure. Got it for the Cub Scouts, didn't we, Dad? But I haven't used it outside yet. Just on the floor in the living room. Oh, boy! This is gonna be great."

"It's not a problem for you to stay until Monday?" Max asked.

The anger she'd seen smoldering in his eyes at the school had diminished, but she didn't want to suggest she stay longer with Ryan in the room, especially after what Max had said. "No, it's not a problem." Tessa took the roast from the oven and placed it on top of the stove. When she removed the lid, the aroma filled the kitchen.

Max and Ryan exchanged a surprised look. Ryan said, "It smells better than Mrs. Clark's."

Tessa shrugged. "It's just a roast and some spices. I've never made gravy, but I guess we can try."

Max cleared his throat. "I didn't know you could cook. Except for pancakes."

"I never said I couldn't. I just don't do it very much. But I can read. I also learned a few things from Leslie's mother. So if you have a carving knife . . ."

Max opened a drawer just as there was a rap on the door.

Tessa answered it. Emma stood there with her left arm in a sling, a basket holding the most delicious-looking apple pie Tessa had ever seen sitting at her feet. "This is for you, dear. I couldn't hold the basket and ring the bell at the same time."

Tessa lifted the basket and took an appreciative whiff. "This looks and smells wonderful."

"Just a small thank-you for taking me to the hospital."

"The hospital?" Max opened the door wider for Emma to step inside.

"I fell," Emma explained. "I saw Tessa in and out with grocery bags this morning, so I called her." The older woman turned back to Tessa. "I hope you weren't too late for your appointment."

"Not too late." Tessa rushed on. "I thought you made your pies for the bake sale."

"I made six. They won't miss one. You enjoy it."

"Shouldn't you be resting? Is your daughter with you?"

"She's waiting for me to come back. Probably standing on the porch watching. She called me a stubborn old woman before I left. I won't admit it, of course. It's the *old* I'm afraid of. That's why I wanted to go to the hospital. But nothing's broken. I just have to wear the sling a few days. You enjoy the pie." She winked. "It's even better with vanilla ice cream on top."

After Emma thanked Tessa again, she waved and left. Max and Tessa watched until they were sure Emma had safely reached her porch.

Then Max said to Ryan, "Why don't you put your books in your room and get ready for supper. We'll talk about what we need for the camping trip while we eat."

Ryan grinned and took his book bag upstairs.

Max took the pie out of the basket and placed it on the counter. "First of all, I want to thank you for dinner. I was going to throw a meat loaf together when I got home."

Tessa closed the door and her heart beat faster without her knowing exactly why. "Ryan said something yesterday about being sick of meat loaf."

Max took off his suit coat and hung it over the back of a chair. His lopsided smile warmed her heart. "I guess he didn't want to hurt my feelings." He paused for a moment. "And I never meant to hurt yours. I'm sorry about what I said in the parking lot. I was out of line."

"You think you know me, Max, but you don't."

"I know you left when I asked you to stay."

"I had to."

"So you said." He exhaled slowly. "But that's water under the bridge." He motioned to the table and the pie. "Why didn't you tell me about Emma?"

"Did you give me the chance?"

"Maybe not when you arrived, but afterward you could have."

Max's nearness in the small kitchen was almost as disturbing as his shuttered gaze. "You honestly thought I might not show up?"

His silence told her that was exactly what he thought. A misunderstanding was one thing; his lack of faith in her was another. She felt tears threaten again. Blast it.

Why did he have the power to bring up this emotion in her? No one else did.

His eyes darkened to tobacco brown. "You come and go as you please, Tessa. I know you're not used to restrictions, to responsibilities."

She planted her hands on her hips, filled with anger because he presumed to judge her. "Do you know of any time I ever let Leslie down? Or you or Ryan?"

"She wished you would write and call more."

"Specifically," Tessa challenged.

"You were late for Ryan's christening."

Her hand sailed through the air. "For heaven's sake, my plane was delayed. What was I supposed to do? Flap my wings and forget the jet?"

Max's voice lowered in response to hers rising. "You could have come in the day before."

"I had an assignment to finish."

He opened the top button of his shirt and tugged down his tie. "That's what I mean about priorities."

"And you don't make teaching a priority?" she demanded. Max's attitude over the years, his nonapproval, had been a thorn in her side. It was about time she removed it. She no longer had to worry about hurting Leslie's feelings. She could go one-on-one with him, no holds barred.

"I'll bet you that apple pie that you go in to school early and you certainly don't leave before you're finished. Just because I seem to control my own hours and I can choose assignments, you think I have a schedule I can adjust at will. I have personal deadlines, I have editorial deadlines, and if I don't turn assignments in on time, I won't get more work. I'm not taking a joyride, Max. I work, just like you."

The silence in the kitchen was magnified by her stillness, his probing regard. He canvassed her face, her defensive stance. "Maybe I do tend to look at your job as one long vacation. We've never really talked about it."

She and Max hadn't talked much at all in the past nine years. Not about anything that mattered. Even when Leslie was sick, they'd stuck to the superficial, to subjects that hadn't caused controversy.

She didn't know if this one would cause controversy or not. "Max, would you like me to stay longer than a week? There's no reason I can't stay a few weeks if it will help Ryan. There's an Economic Summit in Oslo the week before Thanksgiving I have to attend. But until then, if it will help, I'll stay."

"You'd do that?"

"Yes. I can find a room somewhere—"

"No. You can stay here."

"You're sure you don't mind?"

"How can I mind? You're helping my son. Did you see that grin when you said you'd go camping? I haven't seen him this excited in a long while."

Max was happy for Ryan. That didn't make her feel especially welcome, as if Max wanted her, too. The question was—why did she care? She went to the counter and picked up the dish of potatoes. "We'd better eat before this gets cold."

Max didn't pick up the knife to carve the meat. Instead, he tilted his head, his black hair reflecting gleams from the overhead light, and gazed at Tessa speculatively. "It was nice of you to help Emma."

"I wasn't being nice."

A trace of a smile curved his lips. "What were you being?"

He was trying to see into her heart, maybe into her soul. She felt vulnerable and didn't like it. "Emma needed help. I helped. Period."

Max leaned forward and gently brushed a curl away from her cheek. The pad of his thumb across her skin created a squall of emotion inside her as he said, "One tough lady." He didn't say it as if he believed it.

His touch was mesmerizing, and although Tessa knew she should back away, at least move, she couldn't.

"I am sorry, Tessa. I'm sorry I misjudged you. I'm sorry I brought up... the past." He waved his hand across the kitchen. "And I promise for all your effort and agreeing to camp out for the weekend, we'll go to a nice restaurant some time next week."

She wanted to rest her cheek against his shoulder, wanted to feel his arms around her. The wanting was wrong, though. Getting too close to Max was wrong. Somehow the differences that had always been between them felt more comfortable than this tentative understanding.

She leaned away from his touch *and* his understanding. "You don't think I'm going to cook every night, do you?"

"Aren't you?" he teased.

"No way, José. I'll cook when I can, but don't expect it to become a habit."

"I wouldn't expect that." His grin was as boyish and appealing as she'd ever seen it.

But Tessa had a sobering thought. He *had* expected it from Leslie. Every time he looked at Tessa, she wondered if he was comparing her to her best friend. She didn't like the idea. She didn't like it at all.

* * *

"Look, Dad. Tessa has her tent ready," Ryan called to Max as they set up camp Friday evening.

Tessa had agreed with Max that they drive to the state park tonight so they'd have a full day tomorrow. They'd left right after school. The evening air had turned cool and the sun had dipped behind the tree line.

"Ryan, why don't you and I go gather wood for the camp fire while your dad finishes with your tent?" Tessa suggested as she watched Max hammer in the next to last stake.

"I'll go. You don't know what might be roaming around."

Tessa pulled her sweatshirt sleeves down to her wrists and gave him one of her defiant looks. "Nothing very big, Max. This isn't grizzly territory."

"It's still better if I go. Maybe you and Ryan can finish the tent? If you get a chance, you can bring the air mattresses from the wagon." There were two. Max knew she'd probably argue with him about who should use those, too.

"Any more orders, Sergeant?" She gave him a sassy grin.

He shook his head. "Just don't collapse the tent while I'm gone."

She wrinkled her nose at him.

Ryan sidled up beside Max. "You won't get lost, will you?"

"No, pal. I have a good sense of direction. By the time you and Tessa get the tents ready for sleeping, I'll be back."

As Max collected wood, he thought about the past few days. For the most part, Tessa had avoided him. He wasn't sure why. He also wasn't sure why that bothered him or why he was noticing the red highlights in her hair and the vulnerability in her green eyes that she tried so hard to hide. There was something he needed to talk to her about since she was staying, and he didn't know how she'd take it. But Ryan's safety came first and that's what he had to address.

When Max returned to the campsite, his arms full of tree branches and kindling, he laid the makings of a fire in the stone circle and lit it. Tessa and Ryan stood nearby and watched until he said to Ryan, "The forks for the hot dogs are in the back of the wagon next to the fishing rods. Can you get them?"

As Ryan took off, Max poked at a log, then straightened. "Tessa, since you're staying, I wish you'd think before you make suggestions concerning Ryan. With darkness falling, I didn't want him in the woods."

"But he would have been with me."

"That doesn't matter."

"It should. I've set up camp in the Mojave Desert. Have you?"

"No. And it's not on my agenda for this year." He'd meant to give the discussion some levity, but it didn't work.

Instead, she took a few steps away from him. "You don't trust me with him, do you?"

He tried to be as gentle as he could. "I'm not suggesting you don't love him or care about his welfare. But you might not be as cautious as a parent would be."

"Maybe he senses your caution and feels smothered."

He studied her. "Are you giving me advice on how to raise my son?"

She stuffed her hands into her jeans pockets. "I'm suggesting you give him some room to breathe. Holding on too tight is almost as bad as not holding on at all."

"Is this it?" Ryan shouted as he held up a long fork, shining a flashlight on it.

"There are two of them," Max called back.

When he turned back to Tessa, she was on her way to the car, saying, "I'll get our jackets. It's getting chilly."

Max swore as she walked away. No matter how he tried to handle her, he botched it. He didn't know what bothered him most about Tessa. That she didn't need his help, or that he wished she did. She was more than capable at whatever she tried. Leslie had looked to him for advice, for support—physical and emotional. He tossed a few branches into the fire, not knowing why he was even making the comparison, not knowing why Tessa's reactions should be his concern.

Tessa helped Ryan with his jacket, zipping it up to his chin. She was never anything but nurturing with Ryan. And that was the side of her Max didn't understand. She related so well to Ryan, as if some part of her were still that little child. Was she the independent career woman who needed no one? Or was she pretending as some kind of defense mechanism?

After supper, Max sat back in his lawn chair, his feet propped along the stone ring on the side of the fire that burned low. Tessa and Ryan laughed as marshmallows, toasted for dessert, collapsed in their mouths. The white sticky insides lined Tessa's upper lip like a mustache. Max suddenly had the urge to lean forward and wipe it away. Something told him that wasn't a good idea.

He did hand her a napkin. "Need this?"

"Not as much as I need a bath." She waved her sticky fingers and, with a mischievous smile, tapped his right cheek with one of them.

"Looks great, Dad," Ryan said of the sticky blob on his cheek.

Max grabbed Tessa's wrist as she went for his other cheek. "Are you asking for trouble?"

Her grin was impish. "I thought you'd want a matched set."

Her wrist felt fragile under his fingers, so opposed to the tough facade she projected. He released her. "I want you to act like an adult."

"Does that mean we can't have fun?" she asked with a twinkle in her eye but a serious note in her voice.

"Maybe I've forgotten how to have fun," he murmured to himself.

"You have another marshmallow on your fork, Ryan. Bring it here," she directed.

"Tessa . . ." Max warned, though something inside him came alive with her daring.

Ryan gleefully brought her the fork, careful not to let the marshmallow fall off, while Tessa eyed Max. "You think this is so easy. We want to see you pop that whole marshmallow into your mouth without getting messy."

Max looked at the grin on Ryan's face, the challenge in Tessa's gaze, and he decided making a fool of himself might have merit.

Tessa took the white blob from the fork, holding it between her thumb and forefinger. "Open up."

"I never could resist a dare," he mumbled, opening his mouth.

She popped the treat in. His lips felt her fingers' softness and he almost forgot about the marshmallow. Almost. Reminding himself this was just a game, he licked his lips and held out his hands. "See? No mess. I'll have to give the two of you lessons."

Tessa's cheeks looked flushed, but between the cool night air and the fire, he couldn't tell. She sat back, picked up the bag of marshmallows and offered them to him. "Your mouth is bigger than ours. Want another one?"

He laughed and swiped at his sticky cheek with his napkin. "I think we've all had enough sugar for one night. Let's get ready for bed, buddy. We have a lot planned for tomorrow."

"You're going to fish, too, aren't you, Tessa?" Ryan asked.

"Sure am. Unless you dump the boat."

The idea of Tessa wet, her clothes molded to her, quickened Max's heart rate. Why was this happening now? After all these years? He wasn't even sure what "this" was. He'd just have to be careful to keep that boat very steady.

Ryan went into the tent to get ready for bed. Tessa picked up a long stick so she could stir the ashes while Max doused the smoldering embers. His flashlight sat on the picnic table with the beam directed toward them so they could see. He poured water from a five-gallon tank he'd filled after they'd arrived, and gave her a nod.

Tessa stirred the ashes and wondered what she'd been thinking of earlier when she spotted Max's cheek with marshmallow. It had been a spontaneous act, as automatic as putting her pen to paper. He just looked so serious sometimes. Did he still miss Leslie with the same aching grief? Hers had subsided somewhat. Time had helped. Now she remembered the good times much more often than the sadness of Leslie's cancer and her year of treatment.

Max doused the ashes again. "That should do it. Do you have a flashlight?" he asked, setting the water carrier on the picnic bench and capping the nozzle.

She picked up the one on the ground beside her and straightened. "Right here. As quickly as we left, I thought we'd be sure to forget something."

"You did a good job of packing."

She laughed. "I'm used to it. Remember?"

Although Max's flashlight wasn't a flooding beam, she could still see his frown. "I remember."

Eager to find another subject, she said, "Ryan mentioned some type of festival in town next weekend. I've missed it other years. What goes on?"

"It's called Oktoberfest. They have craft booths in the park on Saturday. The softball game on Sunday is usually the highlight. It's a community tradition."

There was that word—tradition—the one she didn't know much about. "The teams are already formed?"

"Nah. Whoever shows up, plays. You want to play?" He looked intrigued.

"I was on a team in high school." It was the only time she'd felt equal to the other girls. They wore uniforms paid for by the district and none of the other girls could run faster or throw harder.

"We mix men and women, and it's usually a lot of fun." He stepped closer, bringing with him the aroma of woodsmoke and pine. "Tessa, I know staying in Jenkins might be hard for you. Anytime you want to leave..."

"Tired of me already?" she joked, though she didn't feel like joking.

His lazy smile surrounded her. "No. But I don't want you to feel tied here, either. Whatever this is with Ryan, I'll figure it out."

Tessa frowned. "You don't need help or you don't want *my* help?"

"Now don't get defensive. I'll take your help. But I want it to be given freely."

She breathed a sigh of relief. "I told you I'll stay a few weeks. I might have to make an overnight trip or two to New York. But unless something unexpected pops up, that's it."

He nodded then glanced around the campsite. "I think everything's secure. The car's locked." Turning back to her, he asked, "Do you want me to get you up in the morning?"

"I'll wake up with the sun if Ryan doesn't get to me first."

Max chuckled, a deep, masculine sound that made her feel warm, even in the cool air. She saw his hands come toward her and she thought he was going to touch her face. But, instead, he only fastened a button on her jacket that had slipped out. "Keep warm. If you need more blankets, give a yell."

"I'll be okay. I have my long underwear." She thought she saw sparks light his eyes, but it must have been the flashlight flickering. "Good night, Max."

He took his hands from her jacket. "Good night, Tessa."

Switching on her flashlight, she ducked into her tent and quickly zippered the flap before she wanted him to touch more than her jacket.

Chapter Three

Ryan's pole bounced in all directions as he cranked the reel, his small muscles working hard, his excitement beaming all over his face. Max fought the urge to help him and move to the other side of the small rowboat, where Tessa was already sitting beside his son, grinning, making no effort to take the rod.

"Look how big he is! It's almost as big as the one Dad caught." Ryan slowly reeled in the bass, the rod bobbing. Turning to Tessa, his expression showing pride in his accomplishment, he asked, "Can you help me get him off the hook?"

Tessa didn't flinch as many women would have when she took the flopping fish in her hands. As she did, she said something in a low voice to Ryan that Max couldn't hear.

Ryan nodded. "Yeah, you're probably right. Dad, we're going to throw him back in."

"What about supper?" Max asked, unable to suppress a grin.

Tessa gave the bass back to Ryan and wiped her hands on her jeans. "We have two already. They should be enough. We brought the instant potatoes, didn't we?"

He was surprised to find Tessa had a practical side, too. Especially since her impractical streak had convinced Max to buy a birthday cake for tonight instead of waiting to have it when they got home tomorrow. "Along with the carrot sticks."

"Are we going to hike this afternoon?" she asked, as she pushed the tackle box aside with her foot.

"There's a marked trail not too far from our campsite." He'd watched Tessa become almost as fidgety as Ryan the longer they'd sat in the boat. Inactivity obviously drove her crazy.

"There's an unmarked trail toward the entrance of the park," she suggested.

Max cast a considering eye at Ryan.

Tessa accepted his silent concern and said, "We can go as far as we want and turn back whenever we'd like. It'll be less trampled, and we'll have a better chance to see some wildlife." She smiled at Ryan. "That would be a special birthday present, don't you think?"

From Ryan's expression, he wholeheartedly agreed. Max had to acknowledge Tessa was right; the unmarked trail could be a lot more fun. When had his life become so static, so safe? Did Tessa always take the unmarked trail?

Max rowed the boat back to the dock slowly, more often than not glancing at Tessa, her smile, the oval of her face framed by sunshine and curls. His gut tightened. A dark, hungry gnawing he almost didn't recognize made him row more vigorously until he did recognize it, and then he rowed even harder.

At the dock, Max threw the line over the post and pulled until they drifted alongside. With hands that were unsteady from the exertion and a rising need he couldn't understand, he held the boat steady. Tessa hopped out and helped Ryan onto the dock. They started back to their campsite, pine needles and leaves cushioning their steps as Ryan chattered about the morning.

Thrusting his hands into his pockets, Max took a wary look at Tessa and wondered why the attraction had resurfaced now.

At the fork in the road, Tessa stopped.

"Problem?" he asked, frowning.

"I have to stop at the office."

"Why?"

"I need to call Emma."

He thought he knew what was coming, but he could be wrong. When he didn't respond, she added, "I'm expecting a package by messenger about the Oslo Summit. When I knew we'd be away, I asked her if I could have it delivered to her house."

"It couldn't wait until next week?"

"I'm doing a preliminary article due in next week. Waiting isn't a word that applies in my business."

No, waiting didn't apply. Neither did roots or commitment. She hadn't changed. Nothing had changed. Tessa's career still came first. Why should he care?

He shouldn't and he didn't.

Ryan's cry broke Max's deep sleep. Awake but groggy, he automatically reached toward Ryan in the darkness of the tent and heard Tessa as she pushed at the front flap. "Max, is Ryan okay?"

"Dad, it's too dark. I can't find you," Ryan cried.

Max put his arm around his son and awkwardly twisted around to unzip the flap to let Tessa in.

She rushed through the entrance and knelt beside the trembling eight-year-old. "What's wrong, pancake?"

Ryan reached out to her. "I couldn't see Dad. It was so dark." He clutched her shoulders and without hesitating she gathered him into her arms.

Fumbling for the flashlight, Max switched it on. "Is that better?"

Ryan nodded, his face nuzzled into Tessa's shoulder.

"Do you want to hold the flashlight?" Tessa asked softly as she rocked him against her.

He nodded again as he took it from Max.

The sight of Ryan cuddled in Tessa's arms touched Max. His son *did* miss a woman's nurturing. He'd instinctively reached toward Tessa for comfort and curled up in her arms. Max couldn't put out of his head the pictures of Tessa mixing the mashed potatoes while he fried the fish, snitching a carrot stick from Ryan's plate, clapping her hands enthusiastically as Ryan blew out all the candles on his cake. She'd bought him a Super Shooter, the latest in giant squirt guns, and a book about dinosaurs—a subject he seemed to be interested in for the moment.

And now she seemed to know how to comfort him in the dark. It made Max feel lacking in some way, yet realistically he knew he couldn't be everything to his son.

It wasn't long before Ryan's eyelids fluttered shut and the large flashlight fell out of his hand. Tessa laid it beside her but didn't switch it off.

"I wouldn't have thought of giving him the flashlight to hold," he murmured.

Her voice was sad. "I know what it's like to be afraid of the dark. A little control goes a long way."

"When were you ever afraid?" Max asked, not knowing if Tessa would answer. Fears were as private as prayers.

She laid her cheek against Ryan's head. "When I went to my first foster home. Before that I'd slept in a room with about ten girls. It was never dark there, never completely quiet. With the foster family, I slept in a room in the . . . basement. It was as black as ink when they turned off the lights."

Curious, he leaned closer. "They wouldn't leave a light on?"

Her voice carried, a little more than a whisper across his son. "I asked, but they said it would run up the electric bill. And heaven knows they took me in to cut costs, not to create them."

The darkness and the silence closed around them. "What do you mean?"

"They had two other children. Taking me in brought in money and gave them a free maid."

"You're kidding. How old were the children?"

"Three and five. I liked taking care of the kids. It was the housework I didn't like. I guess no one really does."

"That's why I still have Mrs. Clark come in and clean once a week." Suddenly more curious about Tessa than he'd ever been, Max asked, "Why didn't you stay with that family?"

He saw the slight lift of her shoulders. "They moved out of state so the husband could take a better job. They were one of my better experiences."

"How many others were there?"

"Three. After the first one, I had a chip on my shoulder. No one wanted a smart-mouthed fourteen-year-old. I can't blame them."

Max suddenly wanted to hold Tessa the same way she was holding Ryan. But he sensed if he even leaned too close, she'd lean away. Confessions at night in the dark always seemed different than disclosure in the light of day.

For a long time they sat in the silence, listening to his son's rhythmic breathing, Max watching Tessa, Tessa watching Ryan. Then Max must have dozed off. When he awoke, he could see light through the tent. Tessa was curled against Ryan's air mattress, the sleeping bag pulled over them both. She looked adorable with her cheeks pink, her hair mussed. Her lashes were long and thick against her cheeks, the dark sweep of them making her skin look creamier.

"Tessa?" he whispered.

"Mmm?"

"Do you want to crawl into my sleeping bag?"

Her wide green eyes flew open.

Max disentangled Ryan from her arms. "I'm going to get a fire going and make a pot of coffee, but if you'd like to sleep longer..."

She rolled away from him, coming to a sitting position. It seemed like a reflex maneuver to wake up quickly. "No. No. I'm awake. I'll be out in a minute." She shook her head almost as a puppy would and ran her fingers through the tight curls, disarraying them more.

Ignoring the desire to ruffle them more himself, Max laid his son in the sleeping bag and gently pulled it across his shoulders.

Tessa peeked from beneath her lashes as she ran her fingers through her hair. The eight-year-old didn't even stir. The tent was large enough for two, but she and Max seemed awfully close, even with Ryan between them. Max's beard stubble was heavy and dark, his hair still disheveled from sleep. The atmosphere in the tent spoke of an intimacy that made her heart race. Did he feel it, too?

She had answered his questions all too easily last night. She didn't know why she couldn't seem to keep up her guard around Max anymore. Maybe she had tried for too long.

Max sat back on his heels. "Take your time getting awake. The sun hasn't been up long and the coffee will take a while to perk." His gaze met hers for an unsettling moment before he left the tent.

Tessa took a deep breath and blew it out. She didn't need time to get awake. His voice in her ear, his warm breath across her neck, had accomplished that. Stopping at her tent for her soap, towel, toothbrush and change of clothes, she headed for the rest rooms and showers. It took her about twenty minutes to feel like a new woman, ready to face Max and her complicated feelings toward him.

At least she'd thought she was ready until she saw him sitting in a chair by the morning fire, staring pensively into the flames.

He watched her drop her towel and toothbrush in her tent before she approached him. "I didn't want to leave the camp with Ryan asleep." He rubbed his hand across his jaw. "I should think about growing a beard for winter. It would save time getting ready in the mornings if I didn't have to shave."

Before she caught herself, she said, "You wouldn't want to hide that chin."

"I wouldn't?"

She covered her tracks. "Nope. How else would I know when you're going to be stubborn?"

"My chin tells you that?"

"Sure does." She pointed to the left side. "You have a muscle there that sort of jumps."

He laughed, and she smiled back, thinking this was a nice way to start the day. The earthy smell of damp leaves and heavy pines, sharing smiles and laughter with someone she— Tessa cut off the thought.

Max pointed to the grate over the low fire. "Coffee's almost done."

She rolled her shoulders and moved her head from side to side. "Good."

"Problem with your neck?"

"I think it was the way I slept."

"How long did you sit up holding Ryan?"

She shrugged. "I don't know." She hadn't only been holding Ryan; she'd watched Max sleep, too.

He pulled the low, folding stool that Ryan had used to roast marshmallows closer with his foot and pointed to it. "Sit and I'll massage your shoulders for you. It might help."

"The cramps will work out. The hot shower helped—"

"Good. Then the muscles will relax even more if I massage them."

Still hesitating, she wondered why. What was the big deal? She was wearing a shirt and jacket. He was only going to knead her shoulders. With a small smile, she sat between his legs with her back to him to provide easier access. His jeans brushed her sleeve when she moved her arm. The cuffs of his flannel jacket teased her hair. When he leaned closer to apply more pressure, she could smell earth and man.

Max's hands were large, his fingers long. He went straight for the knots as if he knew exactly where they were. And she'd been wrong about the massage. It was a very big deal. Her shirt and jacket didn't even seem to exist. The kneading was soothing. He went deeper and deeper, touching more than her muscles. His caring and soothing went straight from his hands to her heart. The sensual stroking made her body come alive.

She didn't want him to stop, but she knew he soon would. The pressure eased, his thumbs made smaller circles, and he leaned away. She closed her eyes for a moment to steady herself, then stood on legs that felt wobbly.

"Thank you," she said politely. "That helped."

He stood, too. "I'm glad. I'm also grateful you were here for Ryan last night."

"I'm glad I could be."

They were standing so close. The air between them seemed to lose its morning dampness and became warm and compelling. She could see deep into Max's eyes and wasn't sure what emotions she saw there. Maybe need, and desire... He bent his head, and her eyelids fluttered closed.

His lips found hers, and she was young again. The desire was there, the heat was there, the wanting that in the past she'd told herself didn't matter was there. She reached for Max and felt his arms wrap around her. And just as she felt as if her heart would leap from her chest and her limbs would never stop shaking, he dropped his arms and left her standing alone.

She opened her eyes, feeling as if her life had drastically changed in a matter of seconds. Max didn't appear to be affected at all. Except...was his breathing as fast and as shallow as hers?

His voice was gruff when he spoke. "The coffee should be perked by now. I'll get the mugs."

As he went to the table, Tessa didn't know what to think...or feel. She watched him pour the coffee, glad he was doing it instead of her. Her hands still trembled along with the rest of her. She had to keep her distance from Max, that's all there was to it.

The following Friday evening, Max poured a jar of seasoned sauce into a bowl and put it in the microwave while Tessa stirred the pot of spaghetti. They hadn't talked much all week. They also hadn't looked at each other directly. Maybe they were both afraid something would happen they didn't want to happen. Like another kiss. He didn't know what had come over him. Gratitude maybe, because the weekend had gone so well. Never mind the surge of desire that had pulsed in his veins when he'd held Tessa in his arms. That had simply been a throwback from the past.

He was looking forward to this weekend, to the fair in the park and the softball games, being out in the air and sun instead of cooped up in the house with Tessa, all too aware of her presence.

When the doorbell rang, it startled him. Answering the back door, he found two of his students on the porch.

The tall, redheaded boy with freckles grinned. "Hey, Coach. Jenny and I are here to talk about the dance. You got the time?"

Jenny, a pretty blonde with a shy smile, said, "I told Kevin we should call first. If this isn't a good time, we can come back later."

Max hesitated. The kids should have had the dance planned down to the last detail before now, but he didn't know how Tessa would feel about the interruption. He glanced over at her. "We're just about to eat supper."

Tessa pulled a loaf of garlic bread from the oven and tossed over her shoulder, "There's plenty, Max, if you want to invite them in. You can talk while we eat."

Stepping back, he motioned the kids inside. After introducing them to Tessa, he asked them, "Would you like to join us for supper?"

Kevin grinned. "Sure."

Jenny jabbed him. "You just had a Big Mac!"

"What can I say? I'm a growing boy."

Jenny shook her head as if she were exasperated with him often.

Tessa laughed and took two more glasses from the cabinet. "What dance are you planning?"

"The Fall Jubilee Dance. We hold it at the fire hall. Coach is the adviser for the sophomore class, so we have to run everything by him before we can do it," Jenny explained.

Max went to the counter and dished spaghetti onto plates. "The committee is late getting organized this year. Very late," he added with a stern look at the two teenagers.

Ryan came running into the kitchen. Seeing Kevin and Jenny he slowed down and slipped onto a chair at the table.

"Washed up?" Tessa asked.

He nodded.

She introduced him to Kevin and Jenny, and Max explained that he taught them in school. Tessa sliced the garlic bread and gave Ryan a piece. He grinned and bit off some of the crust.

Max placed the dishes on the table and addressed Kevin. "So, what do you have in mind?"

Kevin pulled out the chair next to Ryan. "That's the problem. We don't. We can't seem to get any good ideas going. Everything's been done before. We want something different this year."

"If you don't do something soon, you won't have time to do anything at all," Max warned. "The dance is only two weeks away."

"What have you done in the past?" Tessa asked as she brought glasses of milk to the table.

Jenny sat next to Kevin. "We usually do an 'autumn in' theme. Like 'autumn in New York,' 'autumn in San Francisco.' Last year we did 'autumn in Paris.' But this year we're stumped. Do you have any ideas? We just need to come up with a few to take back to the committee. We're going to settle this tonight one way or the other so we can start on decorations. Coach, everything else is done. Honest. Refreshments, people to set up and take down, tablecloths."

"The ideas should come from you." Max sat beside Jenny.

Kevin took a piece of garlic bread from the basket. "You know what we've been getting? 'Autumn in Iowa.' 'Autumn in Canada.' 'Autumn in Kansas.' Not very inspired."

Max chuckled. "You can't say they didn't try."

Kevin scrunched up his face and chewed at the same time. "If that's trying, I should get an A in geometry."

Max knew Kevin did his best, but so far had only managed a *C* in geometry.

Tessa ruffled Ryan's hair before she sat. He ducked but grinned at her. "What if you stretched your theme a little so it's not quite as realistic?"

"I don't understand," Jenny said.

Tessa cut up Ryan's spaghetti with her fork so it would be easier for him to handle. "You could use a place that is well-known, but not real. For example...what about 'autumn in Camelot'?"

Jenny smiled. "That's great. Can you imagine the decorations?"

"What's Camelot?" Kevin looked confused.

"Didn't you ever see the movie or the play?" Jenny asked.

"Or read the legend of King Arthur?" Max offered.

"Must have missed 'em." Kevin started twirling his spaghetti. "But I get what you mean. Like 'autumn in Oz' or 'autumn in Metropolis.'"

"Metropolis?" Jenny repeated.

Max picked up his fork, watching Tessa take a bite of spaghetti. It slipped down her lip. Her tongue came out and swirled it in. He shifted in his chair. "Where Superman became famous."

Jenny rolled her eyes. "I like Oz or Camelot. What do you think, Coach?"

"Either one will work. And if you offer those to the committee, they might come up with others."

Max reached for a piece of bread. So did Tessa. Their fingers brushed. The electricity he felt sparked in her eyes, too. But she quickly turned to Ryan and handed him a napkin so he could wipe sauce from his mouth.

"Coach?"

Apparently he'd missed Kevin's question. "I'm sorry. What did you say?"

Kevin looked at Tessa then back at Max. "I said we're having problems getting chaperons. Do you have any suggestions?"

"Don't the kids' parents want to be involved?" Tessa asked.

Kevin and Jenny exchanged a knowing look. "Teenagers don't *want* their parents around, Ms. Kahill. Don't you remember how you felt in high school?"

Max saw the shadow pass across Tessa's face. He imagined how difficult it was for her not to have a parent to turn to or rebel against. "Ms. Kahill's a foreign correspondent and travels constantly. She's not familiar with teenage dances."

Tessa gave him a thank-you, but-I-can-speak-for-myself look. "I didn't go to many dances, Kevin."

"Why not? I'd think any guy would jump at the chance to take you!" As soon as the words were out of the teenager's mouth, he blushed beet red.

Max thought about smoothing the waters, but he wanted to see how Tessa would handle Kevin.

She simply smiled. "Thank you. I think that's the nicest compliment I've ever received. The truth is, when I was a teenager, I worked every minute I could to save money for college. That didn't leave much time for dances."

"A lot of kids are in that boat," Jenny commented. "We decided to keep the dance casual this year to cut expenses. That way we'll have better attendance."

"Can only parents chaperon?" Tessa asked.

"No," Kevin answered quickly. "You want to come with Coach?"

She hazarded a quick look at Max. "If you need another chaperon, I'll be glad to come. When did you say it is?"

"Two Saturdays from tomorrow."

"If you didn't have a theme, how did you advertise it?"

Jenny looked sheepish. "Just as the Fall Jubilee with a secret theme. We told everyone to come and be surprised."

Tessa laughed and the sound of it made Max feel good. As they ate, he watched Tessa interact with the teenagers. She seemed to relate to them easily. Leslie had always backed away from the students he taught and coached. She didn't understand their rowdiness or rebelliousness. Tessa did. And she didn't forget about Ryan sitting next to her, either. She talked to him and joked with him so he wouldn't feel left out.

After Kevin and Jenny left, Ryan went to the living room to watch a video. Max watched him as he settled on the sofa. "Do you think he'll be like Kevin some day? Interested in girls, involved in school activities, having trouble with math?"

"I'm sure he'll be interested in girls. Now the math..."

Max could hear the smile in her voice and turned toward it. "I know. I should stop worrying so much."

"Why did you let the dance committee wait until now to come up with a theme?"

"This is their dance. Their responsibility. Its success depends on them. I was getting worried, but it looks as if they'll come through."

"Are Kevin and Jenny dating?" Tessa collected the dishes from the table and brought them to the sink.

"Now and then. They're as different as night and day. One minute they're arguing, the next they're talking like best friends." He shook his head. "Teenagers."

Tessa put the dishes on the counter. "I'm not so sure they're any different from adults." Without saying more, she turned on the spigot and went about cleaning up supper.

The autumn sun sent streaks of yellow rays across the field. Tessa dashed her hand across her forehead to swipe a few drops of perspiration. Her skin crawled as Max stared her down, trying to intimidate her, hoping she'd lose focus on the ball and strike out. She never lost focus, not for a second. But Max's piercing brown gaze almost made her forget where she was.

Just as it had all week whenever their eyes met, which hadn't been often despite their being in the same house. Since that moment at the campsite when he'd kissed her, they'd avoided contact. When Ryan wasn't around, Tessa worked in her room. This weekend had been a relief—strolling through the park with Max and Ryan yesterday, watching the children's softball games today. She thought about chaperoning the high-school dance with him. Would he ask her to dance? How would it feel to be held in his arms again?

Concentrate, Kahill. Right now, he's your opponent. She dug in her heels, prepared to swing as hard as she could when he pitched.

Never swing at the first pitch, she told herself. Wait for the right one.

The first ball sailed by.

"Strike one!" the umpire called.

"Come on, Tessa, you can do it," Ryan yelled from the bleachers.

She was glad Ryan was rooting for her. But then she heard him call to Max, "You can do it, Dad. Strike her out!"

She smiled. Ryan was playing both sides of the fence.

The second ball was outside. She called to Max, "You have to do better than that."

His grin grew threatening and smug. "Watch me."

He had a real competitive streak. So did she.

Max wound up. Even from this distance Tessa was aware of the muscles under his T-shirt, the rakish tilt of his cap over his eyes, his masculine stance, supremely evident as he pitched. Max was coiled strength. She pictured him, upper torso naked as he stood on the roof.

The ball sailed by her again and she knew it had been a good one.

"What's the matter, Kahill. Lost your touch?"

Max's deep baritone teased every one of her nerves into tingling awareness. "You just pitch 'em and cut the editorial comment."

This time she was ready.

It was almost like slow motion. Max took a step forward. His hand went back to start the delivery. Tessa was on top of it, her legs balancing her properly, her gaze on the ball, her position perfect for a hard hit.

The ball met her bat with a loud *thwat*. She thought she heard Max swear and Ryan cheer, but she was too busy running the bases to really pay attention. She made it to third, looked up and saw the third baseman waiting to tag her if she moved on. She bent over, her hands on her knees as she caught her breath.

When she straightened, she was staring straight into Max's brown eyes. Instead of the annoyance she thought she'd see, he tipped his cap to her. Then he turned to home plate ready to take on the next batter.

After the inning, Max sat on the bench observing Tessa as she played center field. She was perfectly comfortable with her jeans dirtied from sliding into home plate later in the inning, her hair disarrayed in the breeze, the sun bright on her head. Leslie had been more of an "inside" person. She liked her wardrobe in style, every hair on her head in place. Not Tessa.

She'd gotten to him on the camping trip. Her tenderness with Ryan, her sense of adventure. That kiss. It haunted his nights. Maybe he should start dating again—at least go through the motions. Tessa had been right in a way when she'd said he didn't know her. Maybe he didn't. But he did know he and Tessa were incompatible. She was willful and stubborn, and she lived a life foreign to him.

Tessa was here for Ryan's sake, nothing more. Just as she had been on every other one of her visits. The only difference was that this time she was staying with him instead of with Leslie's parents.

Max tore his gaze away from her to concentrate on the game. A batter stepped up to the plate. He smashed the first pitch, and it soared over the field. Into Tessa's territory. But there was another player coming toward it at the same time, and Tessa didn't see him.

Max felt his throat burn as he yelled. He was on his feet and running before she collided with the other outfielder and hit the ground. Max skidded to a stop as the outfielder, a big, burly man twice Tessa's height and weight, rolled away from her and sat up.

Max crouched on the grass beside her. Her eyes were closed and her skin was as pale as the ball she held clutched in her glove. "Tessa! Tessa, are you okay?"

She didn't open her eyes, and he could have sworn she wasn't breathing.

Chapter Four

Tessa gasped and coughed, dragging air into her lungs. It seemed easier when she tried it a second time.

"Tessa, look at me."

The familiarity of Max's voice made Tessa open her eyes. He looked grim and a little...scared? When she tried to sit up, his arm came around her shoulders.

"Nice, easy breaths. Slow."

Following his directions, she thought about how strong and comforting he felt against her. She could smell sun, grass, Max's masculine scent. Forgetting she had a lead weight on her chest, she basked in the protective feel of him. The male power of him. She closed her eyes to savor the sensations.

"Tessa, are you dizzy? Does anything hurt?"

Opening her eyes, she could have melted under Max's concerned look. Trying her voice, it came out scratchy but audible. "I'm fine. I just had the wind knocked out of me. I couldn't get my breath for a minute, but I'm okay now."

"Ms. Kahill, I'm terribly sorry," someone on the edge of the players around them said.

Max ignored the apology and didn't release her. "Do you think you can stand?"

"Sure. No problem." But as Max helped her up and let her try to stand on her own, her knees wobbled.

"That's it." He swept her up into his arms.

"Max! Put me down."

He strode toward the picnic area. "Not on your life. Not until I make sure you're in one piece."

"Max, I'm fine. Just a little shaky."

"You just ran into a Mack truck and you're too pale. Now why don't you be quiet and breathe easy till we get where we're going."

She wondered if his brusqueness stemmed from the fear she'd been hurt. All she knew was that she couldn't breathe easy with his arms wrapped around her. His hand almost covered her breast, and she was aware of his other arm under her thighs. As he walked, her head bobbed and her cheek brushed his shirt. She'd like nothing better than to lay her head there and listen to the beat of his heart.

What was she thinking? Those thoughts were the kind she'd been trying to avoid! She squirmed in his arms.

"Stay still." His breath stirred the curls on her forehead.

"Where's Ryan? If he sees you carrying me . . ."

"He's at the playground. He got bored around the third inning."

"He's with other kids?" Tessa asked hopefully.

"No, Emma and Scruffy. Emma said she wanted to swing and needed Ryan to hold onto Scruffy for her. Sometimes I wonder if I should get Ryan a dog."

"But?" Tessa prompted, hearing the doubt in his voice.

"But I don't know if he's ready for the responsibility."

Max shifted Tessa in his arms, and her nose grazed his neck. She hadn't felt dizzy before, but she did now, and she was incapable of carrying on a coherent conversation. Max didn't try, either.

A few minutes later, he gently deposited her on a picnic bench. Tessa hadn't been aware she'd caused a commotion, but in no time at all she was surrounded by the man who'd run into her, other players and a group of Max's neighbors who wanted to help. She sent Max an annoyed look. If he'd let her walk off the field, this wouldn't have happened. She didn't like being the center of attention. She got her best stories by being inconspicuous and blending in.

Tessa tried to reassure everyone she was fine and was suddenly overwhelmed by the sense of community spirit that made them all care. Her throat tightened. As they accepted her reassurance and scattered, the player who'd collided with her turned his cap around and around in his hands. "I'm truly sorry, Ms. Kahill. I guess the sun got in my eyes."

She smiled at him. "I want you on my team the next time I play. You know how to go after a ball."

His cheeks flushed. "If I hurt you in any way—"

"No. I'm fine. Really. I'm not going to let a softball game do me in."

The burly ball player clasped her shoulder. "You're a good sport."

"You go back to the game and win. In fact, in a few minutes, I'll join you."

"You're not going anywhere," Max said in a low, even voice.

She stood. "If I want to play ball—"

He pointed to the bench. "Sit down. I'll get you something to drink. Then we'll check for scrapes and bruises."

She didn't sit. "Don't order me around, Max."

He looked as angry as she was determined. He clapped the ball player on the back. "You go win the game for her."

The bigger man looked from one tense face to the other, put his cap on his head and headed for the field.

Max faced her. "I'm not ordering you around."

"It didn't sound like a request to me."

He rolled his eyes. "Tessa Kahill, will you have a ginger ale with me?"

"You don't even like ginger ale."

He shook his head with apparent exasperation. "How could I forget you journalists are so observant? I'll find something I like and bring you a ginger ale. Deal?"

She reluctantly sat on the bench and mumbled, "Deal."

Max couldn't understand the tension still dancing in the pit of his stomach. From the moment he'd known Tessa was in danger, he'd realized he was starting to care all over again. Damn!

He bent over and plucked a can of ginger ale and a can of root beer from the cooler. He flipped a paper cup from a stack in a basket by the cooler, opened the ginger ale and poured Tessa a cup. Then he went back to the table, more concerned about her than he wanted to be. All right, so she'd been on assignment with the troops in the Persian Gulf. Still she'd just had a hard collision and a thudding fall. She might be tough, but she also might be hurting.

When Max returned to the table, he handed her the ginger ale. "Do you want to go home?" Max knew that word conjured up a different meaning for him than it did for Tessa.

She threw him a sideways glance. "We didn't eat yet."

He smiled. She could always make him smile, though more often than not, he wanted to throttle her at the same time. "You're hungry?"

"Sure am. I have to fill up on hot dogs while I'm in the States." When she grasped her cup to take another sip of her drink, her arm rubbed the edge of the table and she winced.

Max set down his can. "What's wrong?"

"Nothing's wrong."

He picked up her arm and was about to pull up her sleeve when she jerked away from him.

"Tessa, if you scraped something, it should be tended to."

"For twenty-seven years I've taken care of myself just fine."

He gentled his voice. "Let's look at your arm."

She expelled a breath and pulled up her sleeve. A scrape ran from midforearm to her elbow.

Max frowned. "That could get nasty. I have a first-aid kit in the car."

Her lips twitched. "And I guess you want me to be here when you get back?"

"If you're not, I'll track you down." It was a threat and a promise, and he couldn't believe the way her defiance kicked up his determination. Macho male meets liberated female. Details at eleven.

Max returned with a plastic box and flipped it open on the table. "Peroxide first."

"So you've done this before?"

He smiled. "More times than I care to count. Just ask Ryan. I'm an old pro."

"Not so old," she mused.

Max took out the bottle of peroxide. "Some days I feel sixty instead of thirty-one."

"It's been hard for you, hasn't it?" she asked softly.

Max's stomach tightened, and he felt the muscle that Tessa had noticed jump. "It's been harder on Ryan. As hard as I try, I can't be a mother and a father."

He unscrewed the top of the peroxide bottle and soaked a cotton ball. "Put your arm on the table." Before she could protest, he said, "It's at an awkward spot. Come on, get your elbow up here. Or do I have to promise you a candy bar when we're finished?" he teased.

"Make it a banana split and you're on."

He laughed. "Your demands are steep. But it can probably be arranged." When his fingers lightly brushed her arm, she started. He was filled with the desire to stroke her, to quiet her, to soothe her, to give her the caring she'd missed along the way. But most of all, he wanted to kiss her again. The wanting was becoming much too powerful for his peace of mind.

"Did I hurt you?" he asked.

"No. It tickled." Her voice was husky and did strange things to his insides. As he lifted the cotton ball, he warned, "This might sting."

She held still as he swabbed the area. He tried to do it quickly. But her green eyes watched him cautiously.

When he finished, he said, "Let it dry a few minutes. Do you have scrapes anywhere else?"

"I'm not going to let you strip search me to find out," she retorted.

The idea made his blood surge, and he turned away so she couldn't see that her words had any effect. He wiped his finger with peroxide and, taking a tube of cream from the kit, squeezed the ointment on the top of his forefinger. "I'll try not to hurt you." He dabbed it on carefully, then took a gauze strip and adhesive from the box. "You don't want the scrape to rub against your sleeve. You can take the bandage off when we get home."

She didn't argue, and he was relieved. When he secured the tape, his knee brushed her leg. He shifted away.

"Max, can I ask you something?"

Uh-oh. He could imagine what was coming. Maybe she could sense his change around her, the turbulent response he didn't want to have. And maybe they should talk about it, take the mystery out of it so it would go away.

"Go ahead and ask."

"Would you mind if we redecorate Ryan's room?"

"Redecorate Ryan's room?" Max repeated. "Why?"

As Max had ministered to Tessa, her pulse had galloped, she'd gotten hot all over and she'd been afraid something of what she was feeling would show. To hide it, she'd decided to ask the question about Ryan's room. It had been on her mind all week.

Pulling her arm away from his hands, she sat up straighter. "Because he's getting older, and I don't think baby animals interest him anymore. He's interested in Matchbox cars. Did you know he knows the difference between a Lamborghini and a Ferrari? And I found out Michael Jordan's his idol. Next to you, of course,'' she teased, hoping Max could see she had Ryan's interests at heart.

Max didn't respond right away. ''Leslie made his curtains and bedspread. She coordinated the colors and picked out the paint.''

Tessa knew that. She also knew Ryan couldn't let go and move on until Max could. She tried to keep her voice neutral. ''It's your decision. But I think a change would be good for Ryan. And I think redoing his room would make him feel special.''

Max gazed toward the playground. ''I thought he'd be better off if I kept everything stable—the same.''

''Stable and the same are two different things.'' Tessa considered her life stable because her work was a constant. But her life was never the same.

He thought about her statement. ''Maybe so. What did you have in mind?''

She lifted her hands in an I-don't-know gesture. ''Nothing specific. Yet. Maybe you and I could go to the furniture store and the wallpaper place. Just to look around and see what's available.''

''His dresser used to be his changing table. And the bed . . . That had been Leslie's when she was a child.''

''I know. And maybe you'll want to keep them. But it won't hurt to look.''

Max's forehead creased and he got a faraway look in his eyes. ''No, it won't hurt to look.''

Suddenly Tessa wasn't so sure. Looking could lead to change. Was Max ready for that change?

Max lay awake in his bed on the first floor. The master suite was situated downstairs in the Cape Cod. He'd bid Tessa good-night at least two hours ago and he was still awake, still trying to figure out why every time he touched her, his body sent a surge of adrenaline racing through him.

She'd looked so at home at the picnic, wiping mustard from the corner of her mouth, talking to his neighbors as if she'd known them all her life. But she wasn't "at home." She didn't have a home. He'd listened to her tell Emma about covering the Olympics in Barcelona. He'd listened to her explain how she'd spent a few weeks interviewing freedom fighters in a country torn by civil war. This was the type of woman who would never settle down.

The pipes upstairs creaked as water ran through them. Then Max heard a steady flow. Apparently, Tessa couldn't sleep, either. A loud thump made him sit up, and he wondered what she'd dropped. Maybe her fall had done more damage than she'd let on. She'd been quiet during the barbecue after the game, after their conversation about Ryan's room. He still wasn't sure how he felt about her suggestion.

The upstairs bathroom was located at the top of the steps, between the two smaller bedrooms. As Max climbed the stairs, Tessa came out of her room and headed for the bathroom. He'd never seen her... undressed before. She wasn't wearing a bathrobe. He guessed the oversize shirt had traveled through more countries than he could count. Its faded blue and white stripes had seen many washings. It only came to mid-thigh, and he wondered if it had belonged to a man before she'd decided to use it as a nightshirt.

The thought made his voice gruff. "Are you okay?" he asked, trying to keep his gaze from straying to her breasts outlined under the soft material.

Tessa backed away from him as he reached the second floor. Her eyes went from his drawstring-tied pajama bottoms up to his bare chest, hesitated a moment, then rose to his face. "I didn't mean to wake you." She kept her tone low, although Ryan's door was closed.

"I wasn't sleeping."

She gave him an odd look, then said, "I wasn't, either. The more I tossed and turned, the more sore I felt. I thought a hot bath might help."

"You'll probably be stiff tomorrow."

She shrugged. "It'll pass." With an impish smile she asked, "You wouldn't have any bubble bath, would you?"

"I finally tossed Leslie's cosmetics last year. Sorry."

Her smile faded as quickly as it had appeared, and for the first time ever he was sorry he'd mentioned Leslie's name. A stab of guilt knifed him. He shouldn't ever be sorry about thinking of Leslie. Or mentioning her.

"I do have some liniment I use when I think I'm as young as the kids I coach and I play too long."

"No, thanks. I hate the smell. I'd have to rub it all over."

All over. For a moment he imagined Tessa without the nightshirt, then forcibly blanked out the image. "I've been thinking about Ryan's room. He has a Cub Scout meeting tomorrow night. We could hit some stores and look around."

Tessa eyed him speculatively. "You're sure?"

He nodded. "I'm ready to look. And if it will help Ryan, I can't discount the idea. He's been talking to you a lot, hasn't he?"

She gave a little shrug. "I just try to stop whatever I'm doing and listen to him when he talks."

Whether Tessa knew it or not, that was the perfect thing to do. "I knew he looked up to Michael Jordan. I didn't know he was so knowledgeable about cars."

"You can't be and know everything, Max. You're only one person."

He felt his sigh from deep in his soul. "I know." He also knew he shouldn't be standing here appreciating Tessa's curves in a nightshirt. Nodding toward the bathroom, he said, "I hope the bath helps."

Her green eyes met his. "So do I."

He left her at the top of the steps, more awake than ever. Maybe a warm glass of milk would help, but he doubted it.

The next evening as Max stood in a corner of the furniture store, he told himself he should have known this wouldn't work. He and Tessa couldn't agree on the color of grass, let alone a new decor for Ryan's room.

The salesclerk peered over her horn-rimmed spectacles at Max as he stood in front of his choice for Ryan. "You think your son would like the bunk beds?"

"But I think he'd love the race-car bed." Tessa stared enviously at the fire-engine red bed shaped like a Ferrari. "Can't you imagine it, Max? This bed, red and blue racing stripes running around the border of his room...wallpaper with race cars. We could paint his dresser red or blue—"

"No!" It came out too sharply, but once out, he couldn't retract it.

"No?"

"It's too...loud." Baby animals to racing stripes was too large a leap.

Seeing a prolonged discussion or, worse yet, a disagreement in the offing, the salesclerk mumbled something about checking availability and headed for the office.

Tessa walked over to the race car, sat and bounced a few times. "It's not loud. It's energetic. Ryan's energetic. It would stir his imagination."

"And keep him awake at night," Max insisted dryly.

Tessa stopped bouncing and pinned him with a glare. "Do you know what your problem is?"

Breaking eye contact, he lifted a wooden lamp on a nearby dresser, examined it and put it back. "No, but I'm sure you're going to tell me."

"New and different irritates you. They throw you off balance."

Max rubbed the back of his neck. There was an element of truth in what she said. He hadn't changed a thing since Leslie died. But that didn't mean Tessa was right about the bed or the wallpaper. "What's wrong with bunk beds and ducks on the wall?"

"That's what *you'd* want," she accused as if he'd just suggested they hold up a bank.

"And you don't want a race car to sleep in?" he threw back, figuring her taste came from her likes and dislikes as much as his.

"I'm trying to imagine myself at eight years old. I was beginning to form my own opinions. If I could have had my own room... Well, I know it wouldn't have been ruffles and pink eyelet like some of the girls wanted."

Tessa was every inch a woman. Yet no one would ever associate her with fluff and ruffles. "You would have picked..."

"Oh, I don't know, Max. I just know a child has to feel he has some say in where he chooses to spend time. He should be comfortable there and feel as if he belongs."

"You're talking about yourself, Tessa. Not Ryan. He crashes at night and couldn't care less about what's on the walls."

"Typical male attitude," she muttered.

"Excuse me?"

"*You* see it that way."

"And you don't?"

"Obviously not."

Frustrated with her and with the whole idea, Max checked his watch. "We have to pick up Ryan. His Cub Scout meeting is about over."

"Let him decide," she said abruptly, propelling herself from the bed.

Max watched Tessa move around the bed and straighten the pillow, wondering if he'd ever seen her sit still for more than five minutes, excluding work. "Do what?"

"Let's bring him in here and see what he'd pick. It *is* his room."

"And you're prepared to accept his decision if he chooses the bunk beds?"

She stopped at the headboard. "Get real, Winthrop. Who'd pick a bunk bed over a race car?"

"*I* would."

She shook her head. "Whatever he decides is fine with me. We'll work around it." She wagged her finger at him. "But just you wait. I think you'll be surprised."

A half hour later, they were both surprised. Ryan did indeed have his own opinion, but it included neither the bunk beds nor the race-car bed.

He plopped on the bed of *his* choice, crawled on his knees and opened and shut the small compartments on the bookcaselike headboard. "Isn't this great, Dad? I can put my baseball cards in here and some of my cars. And all my books can go on the shelf. I can put Mr. Bear up there and my dinosaurs. I really like this one."

Max gave his choice one last shot. "If you got the bunk beds, a friend could stay over."

"Nah. I don't care about that."

"You might later. You're going to have this bed a long time."

"Maybe they make a trundle model," Tessa suggested.

Max had to hand it to her. She was handling this like a good sport. Ryan had nixed the race-car bed right away. He didn't like the high sides.

Max left Ryan on the bed, opening and shutting the compartments, and took Tessa aside. "What do you think?"

She gave him a half smile. "I think he's like you and knows what he wants."

But Max didn't know what he wanted, not where Tessa was concerned. This resurgence of desire didn't mean anything, did it? She was an attractive woman, he was a man, they were in close proximity.... Did he want more than the come-and-go frequency of Tessa's visits? If so, he was out of luck. Tessa would always be coming and going. He couldn't understand why the thought bothered him so much.

"We'll get the bed and the dresser to match. It's something he can grow into." Max's voice sounded gruff. He tried to smile. "If you want a race-car bed, you'll have to wait until you settle down in one place long enough to sleep in one."

"Is that a jab at my life-style?"

When Tessa frowned, the same small dimple in her left cheek that appeared when she smiled became more evident. He was noticing too much about Tessa these days. "No, it's the truth. Let's go ring up the bed."

The following weekend, Max waved his hand at the half-covered wall in Ryan's room. "We should have done what the salesclerk suggested," he said with barely restrained impatience. He should have followed his better judgment instead of listening to Tessa. But he hadn't wanted to argue with her. He could never seem to win arguments with Tessa.

Tessa stared at the middle of the wall where three sheets of wallpaper began to lean crookedly to the left. "Do you always do what you're supposed to do?"

He gave her a dark look.

"All right," she conceded. "We should have made a plumb line. But the room's so small, I didn't think we needed to."

"You do a plumb line so you put the wallpaper on straight even though the walls are crooked. It has nothing to do with the size of the room."

Pushing the curls off her forehead with the heel of her hand, Tessa laid the paper she'd used smoother on the floor. "You're right. I was wrong. Let's do it over."

Her admission surprised him.

"What?" she asked at his raised brows.

"I thought you'd give me more excuses."

She caught the edge of the last sheet of wallpaper and pulled it from the wall. "No point to that. We'd still have a room to paper."

Max almost smiled. Either Tessa was mellowing or...maybe he'd been too critical of her in the past. He didn't stop to ask why, but picked up the wallpaper kit with the plumb line included. "It's a good thing we bought a couple of extra rolls of paper."

"I'm just glad we don't have to be too careful about matching the pattern. That could get tricky."

Ryan hadn't chosen the race-car bed, but he had picked wallpaper with various types and colors of cars sprinkled over a white background. It was lively, but not overwhelming. Tessa had tackled this project as she tackled everything else—with zest and purpose.

Ryan's voice came sailing up the stairs. "Hey, Dad. Are you done yet?"

Max laughed and skirted the furniture in the middle of the room as best he could to get to the doorway. "It will be lunchtime at least."

Ryan yelled back, "I'll come watch you after the Jetsons are over."

Max shook his head and stood beside Tessa at the wall they'd tried to paper. "I don't let him watch TV that often. He's going to take advantage of it."

Tessa used her fingernail to start the second piece of wallpaper and peel it from the wall. "Have you thought anymore about getting him a dog?"

Max took an appraising look at Tessa, as he was doing more and more lately. Her jeans fit her waist, hips and thighs as if they'd been custom fit for her curves. Her yellow T-shirt molded to her breasts all too well. His palms itched and he quickly turned his attention to what she'd asked. "You think it would be a good idea?"

Tessa tore down the last sheet of paper. "Yes. I don't know if he's ready for the responsibility, either, but he'll certainly learn it. It's whether or not you want the bother of training and everything that goes with it."

He grimaced. "The messes?"

She crumpled the paper and threw it on top of the bed. "Barking or whining in the middle of the night."

Max grinned this time. "How do you know so much about it?"

"I read a lot."

Max took the string from the package in his hand and gave Tessa a piece of blue chalk.

She rubbed the chalk along the string as he stretched it. "If you get a dog, he'll be a house dog, won't he? I mean, you wouldn't pen him outside?"

Max gazed into her wide green eyes and instinctively knew she'd felt as if she'd been outside looking in most of her life. "Absolutely not. He wouldn't be a pet if we penned him outside."

She didn't drop her gaze but looked as if she had something else on her mind. He waited.

"You know, you could think about getting a dog at the SPCA. Unless you really believe Ryan needs a pup."

Max supposed Tessa wanted *all* orphans to have homes, even canine ones. "That's something to think about."

He was discovering so many facets to Tessa he never knew existed. Their summer in the Poconos had been filled with activities, talk about the future, work—Tessa had waitressed, he'd run basketball camps for teenagers. She'd told him from the first day she'd met him that she intended to find a job in New York and let that lead her anywhere it could. So they'd played tennis, gone horseback riding, kissed until Tessa would push away and let things cool down. Maybe their time together now was different because they'd both matured.

Tessa tied a weight to the end of the string so it hung like a pendulum. Max pressed the weight against the wall, took the string in the middle, and pulled it back like the string in a bow. When he released it, it pinged against the wall, making a straight blue line.

Tessa was right next to him, wallpaper in hand. He could smell her shampoo; he could almost remember the softness of her tumbled curls. Desire mounted, and he took the roll of wallpaper from her. "I'll unroll. You cut."

Max's gruffness surprised Tessa. A few minutes ago, he'd been smiling at her. Ryan's room was certainly larger than a tent, but she felt the same way she had in the canvas confines. Aware. Much too aware of Max as a man and herself as a woman. His gray T-shirt and black jeans showed off his physique as a suit never could. There was male power there, in the muscles, in the strength evident as he'd shifted furniture to the center of the room.

Max rolled the prepasted paper backwards, with the pattern on the inside, and dipped it into the bucket of water. He waited a few moments, then took it to the middle of the wall where the chalk marked a true vertical line. Letting the paper unroll from the ceiling, he pressed the upper section with his hand, heading toward the middle.

Tessa saw the lower section leaning away from the line. She took the edge to pull it sideways and gave a little yank. But the yank was too strong.

Max swore. She looked up. The wallpaper had come loose and rolled onto his head. Straightening, she saw that the paper had twisted. The pasted side had landed flat on his hair.

A giggle rose to her throat, but seeing the expression on Max's face, she didn't let it loose. "Hold still and I'll see if I can save it."

"What about me?" he growled.

She lifted the corner slowly. "I'll try not to pull out *all* your hair." A few strands stuck as she gently lifted the paper. Moving away from him, ignoring the pull toward him and the urge to wipe the paste from his hair, she tried to attach the paper onto the wall again. When she dropped her hands, it fell. She hazarded a look at Max and saw his lips twitch.

In a monotone he asked, ''Do you think somebody's trying to tell us something?''

Tired of fighting her impulses, tired of keeping a distance from Max, and as if it were the most natural thing in the world to do, Tessa ran her fingers lightly over the pasty section of Max's hair. ''That you need a new spiked hairstyle? Your students would love that.''

The beginnings of his smile disappeared, and she knew she should step back, but she couldn't. Something in his eyes compelled her not to move at all.

Chapter Five

Tessa felt Max's hands on her shoulders—strong, large hands that tempted her with their heat. His brown eyes were the darkest she'd ever seen them. His expression was almost pained, and she couldn't keep from reaching toward him again and stroking his jaw.

With a groan, Max bent his head and sealed his lips to hers. She never expected the fire shooting to every place in her body as their lips touched. She never expected passion to rise up so quickly. She never expected the need that pulled her closer to him.

Max wrapped his arms around her, and "close" took on new meaning. He was tall and strong and hard. She could feel his heart pounding against her breast. Hers seemed to thump in the same fast rhythm, beat for beat. She curled her fingers around his upper arms to steady herself. Max's smell, his feel, his desire pressing against her made her giddy.

His tongue slid along the seam of her lips. She didn't hesitate but opened to him. The thrust of his tongue was demanding and stirred a squall of feeling she couldn't begin to name. She held on tighter.

He thrust deeper and swept her mouth feverishly as if he'd never have enough time if he did it slowly. She wanted to savor every moment, every tingle, every rush of heat. Stroking her tongue against his, she felt him shudder. His hands stroked the small of her back. He was fully aroused and she could feel his need as deeply as her own as she trembled in his arms. As exciting as his kiss was, it made her feel grounded, as if this were where she belonged.

Belong? Her? She thought that was what she'd always wanted—to belong. Yet suddenly the idea scared her. Belonging meant opening her heart, making herself vulnerable, giving up freedom, taking a risk. She might take risks in her work but...

Max pressed her tighter against him, and she forgot about risks, she forgot about being vulnerable, she forgot about freedom and everything but his kiss and being held in his arms. She went pliant against him, raised her arms and laced her hands in his hair.

Max groaned deeply and moved erotically against her. Her heart skipped and her breath caught. She'd never known desire could be like this, that she'd feel so alive, so much a woman, so reckless. His thick hair caressed her fingers as she felt its vitality, as she revelled in its texture.

As her tongue swept over his, responded to his, danced with his, the world and all its concerns blurred. She wanted him; he wanted her. Her body hummed with a primal beat, her pulse raced, breathing seemed nonessential. Max relentlessly discovered every secret of her mouth until no thoughts were the best thoughts and only feelings mattered.

But then all the excitement, the wonderful sensations, the intimacy, were cut off. Max abruptly raised his head, pulled away and dropped his arms. She heard her own gasp of protest as she felt deserted, cold and empty. Opening her eyes, she tried to get a grip on her balance as well as her emotions.

Max looked grim and stricken. "That was a mistake. It never should have happened. I'm sorry, Tessa."

Anger rose inside her because she'd allowed herself to be vulnerable, even for a few moments. She didn't know if she was more angry at herself or at him. She willed her limbs to stop shaking and she willed her heart back to a safe rate. Then she took a deep breath.

Max could see the exact moment Tessa withdrew from him. The passion-induced glaze left her eyes, and he could read nothing from her expression. The change stunned him. A minute ago, she'd been a responsive, emotion-filled woman. And now... She stood straight, calm and coolly composed.

"Yes, I suppose it was a mistake," she agreed. "There's no reason it should happen again. We both know better. We both know nothing can come of it."

Suddenly Max was confused. As he'd kissed Tessa, he'd felt more alive than he had in years. But then thoughts of Leslie had seeped through and guilt stabbed at him. It still lingered. In essence, Tessa had accepted his apology. Ironically, that annoyed him. How could she so easily slough off a kiss that had felt as if it could destroy him?

"Maybe we should talk about it."

"There's nothing to talk about, Max. We'll both forget it. Just as we forgot the kiss at the campsite, just as we forgot those kisses nine years ago.'' She plucked the roll of wallpaper from the bed.

Max couldn't push her. If they talked, he didn't know what he'd say. His own thoughts weren't clear. Her words still echoed in the room. *Nothing can come of it.* Something could come of it, all right. Heartache. Neither of them needed that.

The following Saturday afternoon Max shot baskets in front of the garage, every once in a while glancing over at Ryan, who was racing his miniature cars down the sliding board. Taking the basketball to the far side of the driveway, Max aimed for a hook shot...and missed. He felt as if he'd been missing all week. Ever since that last kiss...

He tossed the ball again and sank it. That didn't make him feel any better. He'd had about two minutes alone with Tessa this week. If she wasn't doing something with Ryan, she was working in her room. She was definitely avoiding him. Well, she couldn't avoid him tonight. Tonight he was taking her to the dance.

Max stopped shooting as Ryan ran over to him. He offered his son the ball. ''Want to try?''

Ryan grinned and took it. ''Yeah.''

As he had many times before, Max showed his son the proper position to shoot. But Ryan's lack of height hampered him more than his lack of strength. Seeing that Ryan was discouraged after three tries, Max swung the eight-year-old onto his shoulders. ''Okay, sport. Sink it.''

Ryan giggled and made a basket. Then another and another. Before he shot again, he asked Max, ''Will Tessa be back soon?''

Max checked his watch. She still had a couple of hours before supper. "I'm not sure. When women shop, they lose track of time." Of course, Tessa could be different. She probably knew exactly what she wanted and where she wanted to buy it.

"But she won't forget to come back home, will she?" Ryan asked, an odd note in his voice.

Max swung Ryan from his shoulders and set him on the ground. "No, she won't. She's going to help us make tacos for supper and then she and I are going to the dance."

"And Emma's gonna put me to bed."

"That's right. You'll probably be asleep when we get home."

"But you'll come in and say good-night?"

"Sure will."

Ryan smiled. "Tessa's birthday's soon. Are we gonna get her a present?"

That was news to Max. He wondered if Ryan had misunderstood something Tessa had said. "Did she say exactly when her birthday is?"

Ryan shook his head. "She said she'd like a Super Shooter like mine for *her* birthday."

"That doesn't mean it's soon."

"Uh-huh. She said it's not far away. Can we get her a Super Shooter?"

Max chuckled. "Maybe we can find something else, too."

"Dad, Tessa's staying a long time, isn't she?"

"Yes, she is."

"I like her here."

Max gave his son a huge hug. "So do I."

Max had rarely seen Tessa in a dress—his wedding, Ryan's christening. There was nothing special about this one, except the way she looked in it. He pushed himself up from the sofa and went to the bottom of the staircase as she came down the steps. The deep green sweaterlike material matched the color of her eyes and looked just as soft and inviting. The flared skirt caressed her hips and swayed against her knees as she reached the first floor. But it was the tiny buttons from her neck to her waist that fascinated Max. They resembled tiny pieces of jade. In a way, she looked conservative, proper, casual, but in other ways...

His heart pounded and he thought again about their kisses, her easy dismissal of them, his heated response to them.

She smiled. "Do you think this is all right?"

Unsure wasn't a word he'd associate with Tessa, but she seemed a little uncertain now. "You look terrific. I bet Kevin will ask you to dance as soon as we get there."

"Isn't he bringing Jenny?"

"Not this time. Supposedly they're both coming alone. The Fall Jubilee doesn't require a date for admission. More kids come that way."

Tessa went to the foyer closet and pulled out her trench coat. Max had seen her ironing out the wrinkles earlier in the week. Did that mean she'd looked forward to tonight?

Ryan skipped into the living room from the kitchen, holding in each hand a chocolate chip cookie that Emma had baked. Emma followed him with his glass of milk.

Max folded Ryan and the cookies into his arms and gave him a hug. "We'll see you in the morning."

Ryan pulled back to look at Tessa. "Pancakes for breakfast?"

She laughed. "You bet." She kissed the tip of her finger then blew the kiss to Ryan.

Ryan grinned and pretended to catch it.

Max felt a constriction in his throat. He stood and said to Emma, "We should be back by eleven-thirty."

Emma set Ryan's milk on a coaster on the coffee table. "Don't you worry about the time. You just go and have fun."

Max didn't think a high-school dance was the place to have fun. But then he looked at Tessa, saw the sparkle in her eyes, the color in her cheeks, and reconsidered.

After they were in the car, he said, "I'm surprised you volunteered for this. You'll probably be bored."

She laid her hand on the armrest in the sedan. "Teenagers are never boring, are they?"

He shrugged. "Our job's to patrol to make sure no one slips liquor in. Or to break up any couple who gets too... involved."

She chuckled. "They probably love that."

"Sometimes I think they do it on purpose to embarrass the chaperons."

"Supposedly their hormones are running wild at this age."

"Did yours?" His question surprised him as much as her.

After a moment of silence, she swivelled toward him, batting her lashes with exaggerated coyness. "Why, Mr. Winthrop, are you asking me to divulge the secrets of my youth?"

He could answer in the same teasing manner; he'd missed her bantering. But he didn't feel like teasing tonight. "Do you have many secrets?"

He thought he heard a small sigh before she said, "Not about that. You heard what I told Kevin and Jenny. I worked as much as I could when I was in high school."

"What about college?"

"In college, too. I won a scholarship, but I had to work to pay for books and other expenses."

No wonder Tessa's life was so focused, that she was so serious about her work. She'd sacrificed to get where she was today. "Tonight you can pretend you're back in high school."

Again, a pause.

"Maybe. Or maybe I can just enjoy chaperoning a high-school dance with the nicest man in town."

Nice? She thought he was nice? Somehow, that wasn't the adjective he'd prefer she use.

The inside of the fire hall had been transformed into the land of Oz, although popular music blared from speakers along one wall. Tessa scanned the room, appreciating the mural of Emerald City taped on the wall, the yellow brick road weaving under the tables on one side, the scarecrow, tin man and lion standing near the refreshment table.

The scarecrow was fashioned from corn husks and old clothes, with a stuffed burlap bag for the head. The tin man's body was a giant aluminum can, his head a smaller one. His arms and legs were aluminum strips. Tessa giggled when she looked closely at the lion. It was a mannequin dressed in a lion costume. It didn't have a mask, just whiskers attached around the mouth.

"Would you like me to hang up your coat?"

Tessa turned to Max. He looked more handsome tonight than she'd ever seen him—the way his charcoal suit fit his broad shoulders, the way his thick brown hair lay obediently across his forehead, the way his eyes sparked whenever their gazes met. But those sparks didn't mean anything. He'd been sorry about their kisses. And the more she thought about it, the more she'd realized they *had* been mistakes. She was leaving in a few weeks to cover the Summit, wasn't she? She'd never been to Norway before and she wanted to travel through the Scandinavian countries while she had the chance. She was planning articles on their health-care system, child care...

"Tessa?"

Her fingers went to the buttons of her coat. As she unfastened the last one, she felt Max's hands on her shoulders. He helped her shrug out of the coat. His hand brushed her neck under her hair. She thought he let it linger there a second, but she must have been mistaken.

Teenagers started to pour through the door. Tessa made her way to the refreshment table where she spied about six adults. As she approached the punch bowl, she realized one of them was Mrs. Barrett. Ryan's teacher was speaking to a gray-haired gentleman.

Mrs. Barrett recognized Tessa immediately. "Hello. I heard you and Mr. Winthrop would be here tonight."

"News travels fast in Jenkins."

Mrs. Barrett laughed. "My niece has Mr. Winthrop for algebra. She's the one who roped me into this." The teacher turned to the older gentleman beside her. "Ms. Kahill, this is Al Weaver, assistant principal at the high school. Al, this is a... friend of Mr. Winthrop's."

The gray-haired man gave Tessa a thorough evaluation and offered his hand. "It's good to meet you. How long have you known Max?"

His obvious interest in her answer made Tessa feel as if she were taking some type of exam. "Nine years."

"I see."

He waited for more information, but she only smiled politely. Being a journalist had taught her the value of pauses.

Finally he said, "If you've known Max that long, then you know how much he loves basketball."

This man was heading someplace, she wasn't sure where. "I know he enjoyed coaching," she said cautiously.

"My point exactly. He's one of the best basketball coaches around. I hate to see his talent go to waste this year as he sits out the season."

Ah-hah. Weaver wanted Max back on board, but for now that wasn't what Max wanted or what Ryan needed. "I don't believe he sees it that way."

As if he didn't hear her, Weaver went on, "We found someone to replace him, but the man's not nearly as good. We could still use Max as a co-coach."

"You should be telling this to Max, not me."

"Oh, I have. Weekly, since the year began. But he's not taking me seriously. I understand the two of you are close. Maybe you'd have some influence."

He understood they were "close"? How did he know that when she didn't even know for sure? "Mr. Weaver, Max does what he thinks is best for his life. I have no influence over that. He might love coaching, but he loves his son more. Right now, Ryan needs him. Sometimes a person does what he *should* do rather than what he *wants* to do."

The wind went out of the man's sails. "I suppose that's true. Of course, family has to come first."

Suddenly Max was beside Tessa, his arm companionably brushing hers. After greetings all around, Weaver drifted toward the crowd of dancers. Tessa didn't know if Max had heard their conversation or not. She also didn't know whether or not she'd overstepped her boundaries. Lately, they were getting more and more difficult to figure out.

Mrs. Barrett ladled a glass of punch. "I was hoping to see you tonight."

Max frowned. "I was going to call you this week to set up another conference."

"I don't think that's necessary yet. I've seen some improvement in Ryan's attitude in the past few weeks. He's more exuberant. Some of his work has improved, some hasn't. Why don't I send you a copy of the two extremes and you can see what you think?"

"You know, any time you need to talk to me—"

She nodded. "Just call. I know that. I know you care, Mr. Winthrop. We will get to the bottom of this. I still believe his biggest problem is not mingling with other children."

Tessa surveyed the large room, the teenagers obviously having fun. "Could a party help?"

Mrs. Barrett took a sip of her punch. "What do you have in mind?"

"Halloween's coming up. We could have a Halloween party at the house and invite some of his classmates."

"It would have to be this coming Saturday," Max said.

Tessa looked to him for encouragement. "Could we do it? It shouldn't be too difficult."

"That depends on how much time you're willing to give it. We have to keep them entertained, so we'd have to plan a few games."

Tessa turned toward Mrs. Barrett. "Are there books for this sort of thing?"

The teacher laughed. "There are books for everything these days. I have a few with games you can use. This would probably be very good for Ryan if he feels involved. Maybe even let him make some of the decisions."

"Let's do it, Max."

He smiled. "If you're willing, I'm willing." He asked Mrs. Barrett, "Are the books and papers at home or at school?"

"I have them at home."

"Maybe I could pick them up tomorrow afternoon." ·

"That would be fine."

Someone tentatively touched Tessa's arm. Kevin stood beside her, a wide grin on his face. "Would you like to dance?"

Tessa glanced at Max. He gave her no clue as to what he was thinking. The shoulder-rocking rhythm made her want to tap her foot and she realized Kevin was waiting expectantly. "Sure. It's hard to stand still to this song."

She felt a few sets of eyes on her as she followed Kevin to the middle of the hall. But once she and the teenager started to dance, they blended in with the crowd.

Max watched Tessa move to the music. He ran his finger around his collar; it suddenly felt too tight. Did she have any idea how desirable she was? He was almost jealous of Kevin, and that was ridiculous. He wished he hadn't overheard her conversation with Weaver. He wasn't surprised Weaver had approached her. Al had asked other teachers to convince him to come back to coaching, too.

When Tessa stood up for his decision not to coach this year, he'd been pleased. But then . . .

He heard her words again. "Sometimes a person does what he *should* do, rather than what he *wants* to do." Was Tessa only helping him with Ryan because she felt some obligation to Leslie? Or had she stayed because she wanted to stay? It shouldn't matter, but it did.

The song ended and another began. The teenagers formed a line. Kevin said something to Tessa. She shrugged and nodded. Next thing Max knew, she was in the line, dancing. She laughed with the kids, misstepped now and then, but looked as if she were thoroughly enjoying herself.

When the music stopped for a moment, Max strode toward her.

Kevin took a step away. "I guess it's your turn now, Coach."

Max said to Tessa, "That depends on the lady."

Tessa's eyes opened wider for a moment. "I'd like to dance with you." She smiled at Kevin. "Thanks."

As the music blared again, Tessa and Max squared off and moved to the beat. He asked her, "Where did you learn that last dance?"

"At a club in London."

Max knew nothing about Tessa's social life. "Do you go out often?"

"Whenever I'm there."

He frowned. "Anyone in particular go with you?"

She seemed surprised he asked. "I know a few journalists. I give them a call when I'm there, and we get together."

As Tessa's hips shimmied in time with the music, Max opened his top shirt button under his tie.

They danced to two more songs, then Max asked her, "Would you like to take a break?"

"Yes. Fresh air would be nice."

"We really should check the grounds to make sure all the kids are behaving."

When they stepped outside, the autumn breeze brushed them. He saw Tessa shiver. "We should have stopped for your coat."

"I'm fine."

He smiled. "Then why do you have your arms wrapped around you?" He took off his suit coat and placed it around her shoulders. It would be so easy to bend down and kiss her.

"What about you?"

"Don't you know men are more hot-blooded than women?" Being with her tonight was making his blood boil when he least expected it.

She laughed. "There's scientific evidence to prove that, of course."

"Of course," he teased. She looked protected with his coat around her small shoulders. He wondered if the material would pick up the scent of her perfume. He suddenly realized Tessa was wearing perfume. He'd never smelled it on her before. Had she bought it just for tonight? For some reason the thought pleased him.

Hundreds of stars liberally dotted the black sky. The moon hung suspended like a golden ball, almost round. Max took a deep breath of autumn air and walked toward the edge of the parking lot.

"It's wonderful out here, isn't it?" Tessa commented. "Too often I'm too busy to see the stars."

"That happens to all of us." Max stuffed his hands into his pockets so he wasn't tempted to touch her. The moon on her face, the slight breeze teasing her curls, urged him to trace her profile with his fingers and play with her hair. He closed his hands into fists. "Ryan tells me you have a birthday coming up. I can't believe we've known each other nine years and I don't even know the date."

She stopped for a moment, then resumed walking. "November second."

"He'll get a kick out of you blowing out candles."

"I won't be here, Max."

This time *he* stopped. "I thought you were staying till mid-November."

She put her hand on his arm, bringing him warmth and gentleness. "I am. I won't go back on my word. But that weekend I have to go to New York."

He remembered. "To meet with your editor."

"He'll give me the inside story on the Summit— where diplomats are staying, that type of thing. We'll also go over future projects."

For the past couple of weeks, Max had put aside what Tessa did for a living. Maybe that's why his attraction to her was becoming too strong to ignore.

Again, he remembered what she'd said to Al Weaver. *Sometimes a person does what he should do.* Suddenly it was extremely important to know exactly why Tessa had stayed in Jenkins. "Tessa, why do you want to help Ryan?"

She stopped and faced Max. "Because I love him."

"That's all?"

She hesitated a moment, then said, "Because he's Leslie's son."

"So, you feel obligated."

"Max, what's this all about?"

"If you're staying here out of some sense of duty or nobility and you don't *want* to be here, that's the wrong reason."

"Even if it helps Ryan?"

"So that *is* why you stayed."

She shook her head. "It's all mixed together. I can't separate one from the other."

Max fell silent, and Tessa wondered why he'd asked those questions. A thought struck her that made her throat tighten. She swallowed a few times. "Are you tired of me being here? Do you want me to leave? I never meant to interfere in your life...."

He took her by the shoulders. "No, that's not it at all."

The deep brown of his eyes, the heat smoldering there, made her pulse gallop. "Then why the questions, Max?"

"Because I don't want you here out of some sense of duty."

She wanted to reach out and stroke the lines on his forehead, the worry around his mouth. But she was afraid, so she kept her hands at her sides. "I want to be here."

The heat in Max's eyes burned brighter.

"Do you believe me?"

"Yes."

A train whistle blew in the distance. Muted music vibrated in the fire hall. Leaves danced around Tessa's feet as the breeze pushed them into the corner of the building. Time seemed to stand still.

Taking one of the curls along Tessa's cheek between his thumb and forefinger, Max felt its silky softness. "I

don't think I've told you how pretty you look tonight.''

No one had ever told her she looked pretty. But then,
she didn't dress up very often. Unreasonably, her lip
quivered. ''Thank you.''

He must have seen the trembling because he traced his
thumb across that lip. He was close enough that she
could smell his cologne, a scent that mixed with his male
essence. The touch of his rougher skin against her soft
lip sent shock waves through her.

She lifted her head, and he bent his.

The kiss was gentle and easy until his tongue slipped
into her mouth. Her knees went weak and she grabbed
onto him. His arms came around her to hold her to him.
His powerful thighs strained against her. He tasted male
and hot.

Abruptly he ended the quick burst of passion by
tearing away and stepping back. Swearing, he raked his
hand through his hair. ''This is wrong.''

Maybe it was time they both faced up to what was
happening. ''Why?''

''Because... Leslie was my wife and your best
friend.''

The loss of Leslie still hurt. Tessa would never forget
their hours of conversation, secrets they'd shared, a
bond that would never die. But Tessa had had plenty of
experience facing reality, so maybe she could accept it
more easily than others, more easily than Max. ''She's
been gone for three years.''

A myriad of emotions played over his face. ''So that
means I should forget all about her and go back to
where we left off nine years ago?'' He sounded angry
and bitter.

"No, of course you shouldn't. You'll never forget her, and I won't, either. She wasn't just my friend, she was the only close friend I ever had. She was the first person I could talk to about my hopes and dreams and fears. She listened and she accepted me for who I was. No one else has ever done that for me. I loved her, Max."

For once Max's guard was down. Turbulent emotions played across his face. "And I did, too. Never once did I wish anything had been different. My feelings for you died when you left, and for the past nine years you've been Leslie's best friend. Nothing more. So what the hell is happening now?"

Tessa lifted her chin and met his gaze head-on. "We were attracted to each other once. Living in the same house, taking care of Ryan together has stirred up the chemistry again. That's all."

Max slashed his hand through the air. "That's all? Have you thought about what it means? Both of us know why it didn't work before. Your career. And that hasn't changed. Has it?"

She had to be truthful. "No, it hasn't."

He took a step away, her honesty driving a huge wedge between them.

The rattle of the fire hall doors opening preceded a burst of laughter and a group of teenagers spilling into the parking lot.

Max's face was blank now, his guard firmly back in place. He motioned toward the noise. "We'd better go back in."

There was nothing Tessa could say to ease the tension. Because nothing *had* changed. But maybe for the first time in her adult life she wondered if it could.

Chapter Six

The burnished leaves covered the grass in a thick layer. Tessa fought a losing battle, trying to rake them into one large pile in the corner of the yard as the breeze ruffled and sent them skittering away. She'd needed something physical to do this afternoon so she could burn off disturbing feelings from last night. As she and Max had made breakfast this morning, they'd hardly said two words to each other.

Tessa worked with renewed vigor, the rhythmic clawing sound of the rake on the leaves somehow soothing her. She had prevented herself from falling in love with Max nine years ago. She'd told herself she could enjoy his friendship and move on, and she'd made it clear to him from the beginning that she'd intended to move on. But had he fallen in love with her? And had she killed that love by leaving and following her dream?

After Leslie told Tessa she and Max were dating, Tessa had tried to forget about Max. And she'd managed to do that very well. Not long after Leslie and Max married, Tessa thought *she'd* fallen in love. She'd been covering the war in the Middle East. So had Phil Evans. One eventful day, they'd both almost been killed by stray gunfire. Nothing had seemed more precious than life, and they'd turned to each other in the midst of chaos. But six weeks later, Phil had moved on—to another country, another war. He'd left her without looking back.

Had Tessa done that to Max?

Tessa stopped raking and gazed up at the gray-blue sky. No, she'd looked back. Often. Only Max didn't know that.

She sighed and used the back of her rake to push the leaves she'd gathered into a high, neat pile. All her life she'd been taught that love hurt. Her mother had loved her father; he'd deserted them both. Her mother had loved Tessa so much she'd given her to strangers to raise. Tessa had connected with the children in her first foster home, but they'd moved away. By the time she'd met Max, she'd been safeguarding her heart carefully for a long time. And when Phil took off without a backward glance, she'd decided from then on to keep herself protected. Her work had to be her life. Losing hurt too much.

Losing Leslie had hurt most of all.

The sound of a car broke Tessa's bout of introspection. Max pulled into the driveway, and she kept raking. But a few minutes later, she couldn't ignore him when he stood in the path of her rake.

She lifted her head and found him studying her. All six foot two of him, rugged and much too appealing in a gray Penn State sweatshirt and worn jeans. Her heart fluttered and she felt like crying. She hadn't cried since Leslie died. It wasn't her usual reaction to a problem or confusion. Activity was.

She raked around Max's sneakers.

He put his hands over hers on the rake, stopping the motion. "Tessa, what are we going to do? This tension isn't good for either of us. Or Ryan."

He knew that would get her attention. She took a deep breath and met his eyes. "What do you suggest?"

"We could try being friends. I don't know if we've ever been that to each other. Even in the beginning, we didn't know each other very well."

Her heart fluttered because his hand covered hers. He emanated a virility she'd found in few men, and she vividly remembered last night's kiss. "And what about the rest?"

He released her and leaned away. "We're adults. We can control what we do. For your sake, mine and Ryan's we have to keep this simple. I'll try if you will."

Oh, she'd try. But he was discounting feelings in his formula. She'd just have to keep a lid on hers and hope that was enough. "I'd like to be your friend, Max."

He gave her a crooked smile. "I have Mrs. Barrett's books in the car. Ready to plan a party?"

"As ready as I'll ever be. I guess for Halloween, we'll have to come up with decorations, too."

He waved to the garage. "There's some stuff Leslie made stored in the crawl space. I'll pull it out."

"What about Ryan's work? Did you look at that yet?"

Max frowned. "It doesn't make sense. One day he's straight on and gets everything correct. The next—"

The object of their discussion came skipping out of the house, a package of Oreo cookies in hand. A milk-and-crumbs mustache hung across his upper lip. "Want some, Tessa?"

She let the rake fall and stooped beside him to wipe away the crumbs. "No, pancake. But I do want you to play a game with me."

His eyes sparkled. "What?"

She pointed to the pile of leaves. "See that?"

"Yeah."

She whispered into his ear, "It's great to mess up. Do you want to try?"

He grinned. "By jumping in it?"

"How else?"

She took the bag of cookies from him and handed it to Max. With a conspiratorial wink at Ryan, she jumped and landed on her bottom in the pile, the leaves toppling over her. "Come on," she called.

Ryan landed close beside her and waved his arms, pushing leaves in all directions. He tried to cover her with them. She returned the action in kind and tickled him. He giggled and giggled, and Tessa thought she'd never heard a more wonderful sound.

Above the ruckus, Max called, "While you two undo everything you've done, I have lesson plans to finish."

Tessa stopped tormenting Ryan. She slapped the leaves in front of her. "You *could* join us."

Ryan chimed in, "Yeah, Dad. Jump. You'll really make them fly."

Max smiled ruefully and shook his head. "Not this time." Crossing to the car, he picked up the books and Ryan's papers and then went into the house.

Tessa had to ask herself what would have happened if Max had jumped into the leaves, if they'd tumbled together, playing and laughing…. If they were going to be "friends," she'd have to set her impulses aside, even imaginary ones.

Monday morning, Tessa pushed the cart through the grocery store. She'd decided to start planning the Halloween party by coming here first. She'd found recipes for cute little Halloween cookies—the kind Leslie would have made. Tessa had never baked cookies before, but how hard could it be to roll out dough, bake it and ice it? She'd also found a recipe for a cake designed in the shape of a pumpkin.

As she passed through the baked goods section, she tossed confectioners' sugar and cinnamon into her basket. Then there was Ryan's costume. He'd said he wanted to be Robin Hood. How difficult could it be to make a hat and green tunic? Max had gotten Leslie's sewing machine out of the storage space and he and Tessa had figured out how it worked. Ryan was excited already about the party. Tessa was going to make it the best Halloween he would ever experience.

At least if she was busy with the party, she'd be less aware of Max. After Max had said his piece yesterday, tension had eased. But she still felt every nerve go on red alert when he came near; she still felt the sound of his voice to her toes. She'd be the first to admit she was confused about what was happening between them.

"Max Winthrop."

Tessa had been thinking about him, but she hadn't said his name out loud. Someone else had.

"*Her* name's Tessa Kahill."

Tessa craned her neck and could just see over the boxes of cake mix into the next aisle. Nothing could keep her from eavesdropping.

A black-haired woman said, "They were at the dance together. She acted like a teenager, dancing with the students. He just stood and watched her. He was probably mortified. I hear she was a friend of his wife's. And she's living with him!"

A frosted-haired lady shook her head. "I heard she's only staying a few weeks. She's a reporter or something and travels around the world. Imagine."

"I'm imagining, all right. He's a red-blooded male; she's a red-blooded female. You can't tell *me* there's no hanky-panky going on."

How dare these women judge Max? How dare they butt into his private business? Tessa opened her mouth, then closed it again. Max would hate it if she caused a scene. She wondered what other rumors were spreading across town. Suddenly she remembered Al Weaver's statement that he knew she and Max were "close." What did he think he knew?

Her cart rattled as she pushed it down the aisle to finish her shopping. She'd better not end up in the same check-out line as those two women or she'd be tempted to set them straight. Nothing was going on between her and Max. Nothing at all.

Later that evening, Tessa finished reading a story to Ryan and closed the book. He'd snuggled up against her and didn't seem eager to move away. She'd tried to put the supermarket conversation she'd overheard out of her mind, but it bothered her. Should she tell Max about it? Or should she pack up her bag and computer and move to a motel?

Ryan stirred against her. What would be best for him?

Squiggling sideways, he took his bear from atop his new bed.

She kept her arm loosely around him. "How do you like your new room now that you've been sleeping in it awhile?"

He stuffed his bear farther into the crook of his arm. "It's great. I dream about driving all those cars." He pointed to the walls.

"Maybe on Saturday you can show your friends your room."

"I can?"

"Sure. Friends like to hang out in each other's rooms."

When Ryan didn't respond, she asked, "Are you looking forward to your party?"

He grinned. "I can't wait to be Robin Hood. Jimmy said he's gonna be Batman. His mom made a cape and everything!"

Jimmy and five other seven- and eight-year-olds would be invading the house Saturday evening. Ryan had decided himself who he wanted to invite. "Do you and Jimmy play together much at school?"

Ryan shrugged. "Sometimes."

She could tell she wasn't getting anywhere with that angle. "You know, you don't have to wait to have a party to invite someone over. Maybe sometime Jimmy or someone else can come and stay overnight. Wouldn't that be fun?"

Ryan shrugged again.

"Friends make life more fun."

"I have you and Dad," Ryan mumbled into his bear.

"Sure, you do. But it's nice to have all kinds of different friends to do things with—go to the movies, play games."

He raised his head. "Do you have lots of friends?"

She had acquaintances. People who brought in her mail, met her at a club, discussed work. "I don't have too many friends because I move around so much. But I had a very best friend once—your mom."

Ryan squinted his eyes as if he were trying to remember Leslie. "She was pretty. Dad has pictures."

"She was pretty and wonderful and she loved you very much." Tessa wished Ryan could have known Leslie longer, could remember her better.

Ryan regarded Tessa carefully for a moment, and she thought he was going to say something, but he didn't. She held him a little tighter. "Honey, if there's anything you ever want to talk about, anything that's bothering you, you know you can tell me or your dad."

Ryan avoided her gaze and played with the ribbon on his bear.

Tessa waited but when he still said nothing, she didn't want to push him. Kissing the top of his head, she moved away. As she stood by the side of the bed, Ryan scooted down under the covers. She adjusted them under his chin. "Good night, pancake. I'll see you in the morning." She switched on the night-light on his chest of drawers, turned off the overhead light and closed his door.

Max heard Tessa come down the stairs as he emptied the dishwasher. He knew every creak in the house. He knew the sound of Tessa's footsteps. He also knew the smell of her shampoo, the softness of her hair, the crinkle of her nose right before she smiled. He didn't know if his "friendship" idea was working for her, but it wasn't working for him. He'd thought the decision would be enough, that the attraction would abate, that he could treat her as he treated . . . a colleague. Wrong.

She'd been quiet this evening. He suspected something was bothering her. Was she ready to fly off to somewhere new? Was she getting bored? He'd better prepare himself for that because it could happen at any time. He was surprised she'd lasted in Jenkins this long. He glanced at the baking supplies she'd left stacked on the counter. He had to admit she was giving Ryan her all. He should be grateful for that.

Tessa's sneakers squeaked on the tile as she walked across the kitchen. She held out her hand for a dish.

Max smiled and gave it to her. She stowed it in the cupboard where it belonged.

"Ryan all tucked in? He appreciates hearing a story read by someone other than me."

"Max, do you think I should find a room somewhere or move into a motel?"

He felt as if she'd sideswiped him. "Where did that come from?"

She closed the cupboard that held the dishes. "Maybe my being here is confusing for Ryan. When I leave—"

The phone's shrill ring interrupted. It rang again.

Max snatched up the phone with a sharp, "Hello."

After listening for a few moments, he said, "Sure, that's not a problem." He kept his eyes on Tessa as she put away the glasses. Her sweatshirt was full and loose, but Max could envision her curves all too well from when he'd felt her pressed against him. "I'll see you at seven-thirty." He hung up, ready to return to his discussion with Tessa.

She shoved a juice glass onto the shelf and closed the door. "You have an appointment in the morning?"

"The principal wants to see me," he said quickly, wanting to get back to the subject of her moving out.

She glanced at him sideways as she took the silverware from its holder. "Do you know why?"

Something in her voice caught his attention. "No. It could have something to do with a student, scheduling, basketball."

"And it could be something else," she mumbled, opening the drawer.

"Like what?"

The forks clanked into place. "Like me living in your house."

"You can't be serious!"

She separated the spoons from the knives, still without looking at him. "I overheard two women at the grocery store today. It was as if they were talking about some scandal. High-school teacher lives with reporter."

"You're overreacting."

"Not if there are rumors about you and me flying all over town. Even Mr. Weaver said..."

Max took the remaining silverware from her hand, dropped it in the drawer and closed it. "What did Al say?"

"That he knew we were 'close.' How does he know anything?" Her gaze met Max's and he could see the worry there.

He blew out a breath and hooked his thumbs in his back pockets so he wouldn't be tempted to caress her face and soothe the worry away. "This is Jenkins, Tessa. It's a small town. People talk. Ten percent of what they repeat is true. Ninety percent isn't. Everyone knows that."

"Maybe your principal doesn't. Max, you're a teacher. I don't want to put your reputation or your job in jeopardy."

Tessa was worried about him. It was an unfamiliar feeling. No one had cared or worried since Leslie... "Is this why you were thinking about moving out?"

She turned and picked up a towel lying on the counter. "I don't want to cause problems. For you or Ryan."

He wished she'd just be still. But that wasn't Tessa. "The best thing for Ryan is for you to be here. Can't you see that?"

She folded the towel in half, then in half again. "But if he gets too attached and I leave..."

"He's already attached, Tessa. In between your visits, he talks about you often. He looks forward to your coming the same way he looks forward to Christmas. I wonder if you aren't more afraid that *you're* getting too attached to him. Do you want to move out?"

She hesitated, and he saw her grip tighten on the towel.

"You're starting to feel closed in, aren't you?" He moved a step closer to emphasize his question. "We're taking up too much of your time, aren't we? Cutting into your work, keeping you tied down. That's what family does, Tessa."

A hurt look came into her eyes. "I wouldn't know."

He reached for her, but she backed away. The silence separated them as much as the physical distance she'd put between them. Wasn't that best for both of them?

Maybe so, but he didn't like it. He couldn't keep the edge from his voice. "You don't have to help with this. I know you probably have something you need to do. By tomorrow evening, we'll know whether your living here is an issue. We can deal with it then." It unsettled him to think about Tessa moving out. But he'd better get over it. She'd be leaving soon, anyway.

He returned to the dishwasher and pushed in the top rack. By the time he lifted a casserole from the bottom one, Tessa was gone.

Tessa worked on Ryan's costume the next day while waiting for Max to get home from school. The sewing machine was temperamental, and she'd ripped out more seams than she'd sewn in. But then her patience was in short supply today. She was anxious to learn about Max's meeting.

She'd asked herself over and over if she felt crowded, if she was resentful of Max and Ryan cutting into her work time. Neither was a problem. She had plenty of time all day to work. Being with Max and Ryan in the evenings felt "right." That's what scared her. Since when had staying in one place felt "right"? And when she thought about leaving, she had this sinking feeling in her stomach she didn't understand.

She pulled the forest green material away from the needle and examined the puckered cloth. Damn! According to the instruction book, she didn't have the tension set right.

Hearing the back door open, Tessa went still. She recognized the thump of Max's briefcase on the counter and followed the sound of his footfalls as he came into the living room.

"Where's Ryan?" he asked as he came around the sofa and gazed at the Halloween decorations that had been stored in the garage. A scarecrow sat on the hearth next to the fireplace. A stuffed black cat perched on the television. Flat plastic pumpkins hung in the windows. He didn't miss the Indian corn arrangement on the mantle.

Tessa's gaze traveled up Max's long legs to the wide breadth of his shoulders. He was wearing slate-blue dress slacks and a blue-and-gray pullover sweater. His gray-striped tie settled in the V neck was still knotted and straight. She didn't think he'd ever looked more handsome...or more serious. She was almost afraid to hear what he had to say. Suddenly she realized she didn't want to leave. That thought almost panicked her because of its hidden ramifications.

Remembering he'd asked a question, she laid the tunic on the cushion next to her. "Ryan went with Emma to pick up Scruffy at the groomer's."

"Even trimmed, that dog still looks like a mop," Max said ruefully as he paced restlessly across the room and picked up the black cat.

"Well?" she prodded.

He set the cat back in its place. "You were right about rumors. The principal asked me about you."

She couldn't seem to find her voice. When she did, it was husky. "Should I leave?"

His brown gaze bored into her. "Do you want to?"

"No." The word came out in a rushed puff and hung in the silence that followed. She couldn't be sure, but some of the lines on Max's face seemed to relax with her answer.

He loosened his tie and tugged it open, letting it hang around his neck. "Weaver attended the meeting, too. I told them both that you were a friend of the family, and you're helping me with Ryan."

"They accepted that?"

"Why shouldn't they? It's the truth!"

It was, but maybe not the whole truth. "Yes, I know. But there still might be talk."

Max savagely pulled the tie from around his neck. "Look, Tessa, you know nothing's going on between us. I know it and now the powers-that-be know it. I told them I had to do what was best for Ryan and for the time at hand, your being here is what's good for him. Anyone who has a problem with that can talk to me face-to-face."

He was making it perfectly clear he wanted her in his house for Ryan's sake, not his. What else could she expect? She'd left him once before, and he expected her to leave again. And she would be leaving in a few weeks.

Wouldn't she?

"It's probably a good thing I'm going to New York next weekend. The word will get around, and people will realize I'm not here to stay."

Max didn't seem relieved. "When are you leaving?"

"Early Friday morning."

"And when are you coming back?"

"Sunday."

"Have you told Ryan yet?"

"Yes."

"And?"

She felt as if he were giving her the third degree. "He didn't ask any questions. I think he's excited about the Halloween party and that's foremost in his mind."

Max looked around the room again at the decorations Leslie had either bought or made. "Do we have everything we need?"

"I'd like to buy pumpkins to make jack-o'-lanterns."

He brought his attention back to her. "I know a farm on the outskirts of town that sells apples, cider and pumpkins. We could take a ride after supper. Ryan would probably like that."

But what about you? she asked silently. "I've been cooped up all day with this. I could use the fresh air."

He frowned. "Tessa, if you'd rather be working..."

"I didn't say that, Max. A ride in the country will be nice."

He gazed at her speculatively for a moment. "I'll go change. Anything started for dinner?"

She waved at the sewing machine. "Sorry. I didn't have time."

Max crossed to the hallway. "We'll stop and get fast food. Ryan would eat it every night if I'd let him."

As he walked down the hall, Tessa sank deeper into the couch, letting her head rest against the back. He didn't expect anything of her. In a way, that made her sad.

Max stepped into the kitchen Thursday after school and stepped into chaos. Three pumpkins sat on the table, their tops crookedly chopped off. Scoopfuls of pumpkin pulp and seeds lay on last night's newspaper, making it soggy. The smell of burnt something lingered in the air, and he thought traces of smoke hung in the corner above the stove. The kitchen window was open, and cold air blew in. But it was the flour that really caught his attention. It was everywhere. Across the pastry cloth spread on the counter, in bold fingerprints on the cupboards, across the front of the sink, but most of all—smudging Tessa.

She stood at the mixer, dipping a spatula into... He didn't know what it was. It was white and drippy. Her jeans were covered with white splotches where she'd wiped her hands.

As Max closed the door, Ryan ran into the kitchen. "Tessa, somethin's wrong! One side's longer than the other. And it's so long. And it waves on the bottom. And it won't stay up!''

When Tessa turned toward Ryan, she looked... devastated. "Oh, Ryan. Come here. Let me see."

She crouched down in front of him. The costume, if one could call it that, had slipped off one shoulder. One sleeve was definitely longer than the other. The seams puckered and the bottom hem looked like a drunken scallop.

"It's like a dress," Ryan wailed.

"That's because it's long," Tessa explained. She slipped her belt from her jeans and held it around Ryan's waist for effect. Avoiding Max's gaze, she muttered, "That's worse."

Ryan looked up at her with wide brown eyes. "Do I hafta wear it?"

Max intervened. "Come here and let me see." Hunching down, he folded the longer sleeve under and settled the tunic up on Ryan's shoulders. "Maybe if you wear a shirt under it—"

"Honey, you don't have to wear it. I guess I'm just not a very good seamstress. I thought I could do it without a pattern."

"What am I gonna wear for the party? I told everybody you were makin' me Robin Hood."

Max held Ryan's shoulder. "We can go buy a costume."

Ryan's lower lip trembled. "That's not the same."

"I know it's not. But Tessa did her best and—"

Tessa crouched down again next to Max. "Honey, I *will* make you a costume. Let me think about it until after supper, okay?"

Ryan hesitated for a moment, then solemnly nodded.

Max stood, his knee brushing Tessa's. A jolt of current forked through him. *Friends,* he repeated to himself. *Simply friends.*

Tessa straightened, too, and rumpled Ryan's hair. "Go take that off. Toss it into my room on the bed." As Ryan left the kitchen, she avoided Max's gaze and went over to the mixer.

Last night, he couldn't believe his relief when she said she'd stay in his house. Yet he'd told himself it didn't mean anything. She was doing it for Ryan. "I know how much time you put into that."

"It wasn't my best, Max. I don't know why you said it was. If I had more time, I could do it right. Just like I could do the jack-o'-lanterns and the cookies and the icing...." Her voice broke.

Max had never seen Tessa in this state. She was actually close to tears! He'd always thought of her as composed and confident and not giving a damn. Taking her by the hand, he tugged her toward the living room.

"Max, what are you doing?"

"We're going to talk." When they reached the sofa, he gave her a little push and she sat. "Tell me what happened today."

Tears welled in her eyes as she looked at the sewing machine sitting on the coffee table. She blinked fast as Max stretched his arm along the sofa behind her. "Not much. After I finished his costume, I had to run to the store again. I didn't know what a pastry cloth was. The dough wouldn't stick together and I guess I rolled the cookies too thin because the first batch burned. The bowl of icing got too hard to spread because I was working on the pumpkins, so I guess I added too much milk the second time and... Oh, Max. I was trying so hard to make this special for Ryan like Leslie would have...."

Max couldn't keep his arm from coming around her shoulders. "You're not Leslie."

She sucked in a breath and paled. "Don't I know it. You're used to the way she cooked, the way she took care of Ryan—"

"You can't take Leslie's place."

Tessa moved away from him. "No, I can't and I was stupid to try."

He stilled, shaken by her words and their underlying implication. "*Are* you trying to take Leslie's place?"

Chapter Seven

Tessa's chin came up and fury blazed in her eyes. "Are you trying to be purposely cruel?"

"No. I want to know why you're so upset. The Tessa I know wouldn't give a damn about all this. She'd cut her losses and move on."

"I told you. I wanted to make Halloween special for Ryan."

"And?"

She glared at him defiantly, but her lower lip quivered. "And you have certain standards. I can see it in your eyes. You expected Leslie's meals to be perfect and they were, you expected her to be a wonderful mother and she was, you knew she'd never embarrass you and she didn't."

"You're competing with her," he concluded.

"I am not!" Tessa wrapped her arms around herself.

"Yes, you are. You've never done that before. Why now?" Tessa was more complicated than any woman Max had ever known. He was filled with the need to understand her in a way he'd never tried to before.

She scooted away from him, toward the front of the sofa. "This is getting us nowhere."

"Running away again, Tessa?" An old hurt pierced his heart.

She looked angry enough to slap him. "I don't know what I'm doing. All I know is I've tried my damnedest to be what you and Ryan need—"

Max pushed the hurt away. "And you've done a terrific job." He hadn't expected to say that, but he realized he'd never meant anything more.

Tessa seemed stunned. "You're just saying that to make me feel better."

He could kick himself for letting the weeks go by without telling Tessa how much he appreciated everything she did. He'd tried so hard not to put any demands on her, not to expect too much, not to get too close. "I'm saying that because it's true. You're great with Ryan. You've supported him and talked with him and played with him in the past few weeks in a way that I can see has made a difference. You've pitched in and helped around here with meals and shopping in a way I never knew you could. And when do you think you embarrassed me?"

"By dancing with Kevin at the dance, staying here with you and causing gossip..."

She had a smudge of flour on one cheek. He stroked it with his thumb and pushed a few of her curls behind her ear. "Oh, Tessa. Chaperons dance with kids all the time. I was proud of how you could communicate with Kevin and Jenny and fit right in at the dance. And as far as you staying here, I'm too old to care what the town thinks as long as I know I'm doing what's right for me."

A few tears spilled over onto her cheeks, and she ducked her head.

Max lifted her chin with his knuckle. "I've been a fool not to show you some appreciation."

She waved toward the kitchen. "I thought you'd be angry that all this work didn't turn out right for Ryan."

"We'll figure out something. Tessa, you're not Leslie. Don't try to do everything as she would have. Do what *you* want." He glanced at the sewing machine. "But I don't think you should try to sew another costume."

She gave him half of a smile and attempted to wipe away her tears.

He did it for her, relishing the feel of her soft skin, practically drowning in her beautiful green eyes. Tessa was a Siren, drawing him to her with a mysterious song. She always had been.

He leaned toward her with the word *friendship* focused in his mind. He reminded himself of it again right before his lips met hers. He kept the kiss quiet, chaste, but the singeing heat of their lips meeting surged through his blood like liquid flame. He laced his fingers in her hair and stroked. The gesture was meant to soothe but with each pass through her hair, he wanted to take her tighter into his arms, pull her over onto his lap, feel her body....

He didn't attempt to slip his tongue between her lips and the kiss couldn't have lasted more than a few seconds, but it was no less arousing than any other they'd shared.

When he leaned away, Tessa pulled in a breath and expelled a sigh.

"Friends?" he asked, reminding himself again.

She looked confused for a moment, then nodded. "Friends."

And at that moment Max knew he was lying to himself.

Six little boys chattered and laughed and giggled as they scrambled from kitchen chair to kitchen chair set up in the middle of the living room. Tessa stopped the tape of children's songs, and Jimmy ended up on Ryan's lap while Ryan yelled, "No, no. It's *my* chair!"

Standing at the tape player, Tessa called to Jimmy, "You can help me play the music."

Jimmy's pout turned into a smile as he ran up to Tessa. She wondered what she'd do with the next four boys who lost their place in the game.

Max came to stand in back of her. She felt his presence; she felt his heat. She remembered his "friendly" kiss and almost forgot about Jimmy and the music. "Okay, Jimmy, stop it again."

This time Ryan didn't get a chair.

Max said at her ear, "Pizza's here. If we're going to roast hot dogs in the fireplace, we'd better get them started."

His breath was a hot slash along her neck. His cologne, freshly applied after his shower, wove around her. If she leaned back, his hard chest would be a sturdy bulwark, the place where she'd most like to lay her head. The thought startled her. Since when had she progressed to that fantasy?

As Ryan ran over to the tape player, his mouth turned downward into a frown because he hadn't won the game. Max slung an arm around each of the boys. "You can help me put the hot dogs on the skewers." He winked at Tessa. "As they lose their chairs, send them out to me."

Tessa smiled. Max was wonderful with kids—there was no doubt about it.

After Thursday had turned into such a disaster, she'd thought about doing the party "her" way. Talking with Ryan about possibilities for costumes, she'd fashioned a robot costume out of cardboard boxes and tinfoil. He'd seemed pleased, wearing it around the house for most of the day. Then, of course, like the other boys, he'd discarded it a half hour after his friends had arrived. Costumes got in the way of serious play.

Tessa had found a piñata in a specialty store in New Haven and it had been a terrific icebreaker. Max had attached it to a rafter in the basement and each boy took a turn swinging and finally scrambling to fill his Halloween bag with the treats that had scattered over the floor. From that they'd progressed to pin the tail on the donkey, seeing who could spray string confetti the farthest, and musical chairs. Tessa had decided kids would rather have pizza than a fancy pumpkin cake. Ryan had asked if they could roast hot dogs in the fireplace.

Tessa watched the boys push another chair from the circle. One of Ryan's classmates claimed the last chair, and she presented him with a miniature car for his prize.

Ryan and his classmates enjoyed cooking the hot dogs more than eating them. They devoured the pizza and the cookies with equal enthusiasm. Max had helped her with a batch of icing that had finally turned out to be the appropriate consistency.

The party almost over, the boys curled on the floor in front of the fireplace, finishing cookies and soda. Max sat on the sofa, his legs stretched out in front of him, the flames leaping in the fireplace and casting shadows across his face. Tessa felt warm, cozy...and strangely content, not something she felt often.

When the phone rang, Max picked it up, listened, then above the boys' chattering said to Tessa, "You'd better take it in the kitchen so you can hear."

Setting her plate on the hearth, she went to the other phone. She was used to getting calls any place, any time. But Max's brows were raised as if he were wondering who could be calling her now. When she picked up the receiver and heard Dan Holloway's voice, she smiled.

In the living room, Max heard her, "Hi! How are you?" and he replaced the receiver on its stand.

It was a man's voice on the line. He shouldn't be surprised. After a few minutes of foot tapping, he suggested to Ryan, "Why don't you show your friends your room?"

"And all my cars?" Ryan asked.

"Sure. The boys' parents will be here soon to pick them up."

All six boys scrambled to their feet, and with Ryan leading, clomped up the stairs.

Max figured they'd be occupied for at least five minutes so he could find out what was happening with Tessa.

When Max entered the kitchen, Tessa had the phone cradled against her cheek and she was smiling. "I know your photo spreads are the best. And I'd love to fly down to Brazil with you." She quickly glanced at Max, then away. "But I can't."

Max suspected this man on the other end of the line was giving her all the reasons she should join him.

"I know the rain forest is getting more and more press. How long will you be there?...That's all? So you'll be back in New York next weekend?"

Max didn't like the eagerness in her tone or the degree of friendliness. "I'll be in town for a meeting with Williamson... Yes, I'll be checking in sometime Friday. Give me a call at the Bennington if you're back."

Max watched her as she listened intently to the speaker on the other end. Her smile disappeared and she frowned. "I know it's a good opportunity. But there's no time limit. You can write it up yourself." She laughed at some comment he made and teased, "Get a spellchecker."

Max's stomach tightened at her easy laugh, her warmth to another man.

After a few more minutes of conversation, she hung up, pensively putting the phone on its cradle. Remembering he was there, she asked him, "You left those whirlwinds alone?"

"For a few minutes. Ryan has enough cars to keep them all occupied for a short while." Max motioned toward the phone. "It sounds as if you turned down an assignment you wanted."

She shrugged, a Tessa shrug, sort of a half lift of her shoulders. "There are lots of assignments I want. I can't take them all."

Max had to ask, "It's not a once-in-a-lifetime chance?"

"No. The Summit is. This isn't."

That was a subtle warning. She was telling him Ryan came first now, but come mid-November, she'd be gone. That's what he expected, wasn't it?

Tessa picked up a cookie from the plate on the counter and took a small bite. "I got a call yesterday from Mark Thompson at WHBT TV in New Haven. He wants to interview me on their morning talk show."

Tessa broke off another piece of cookie and popped it into her mouth.

When her lips closed around it, Max's blood heated up as he remembered the taste of her. "How did they know you were around?"

"When I was doing research last week, I called someone I know at the station."

"You have connections everywhere."

"I have to in my business."

He willed his blood to cool, his pulse to slow down. "Are you going to do it?"

"Monday morning. After I get back from New York. I wondered if you and Ryan would like to go along to the taping, see the inside of the station and what goes on."

Max's first inclination was to say "No." But then he realized it could be a valuable experience for Ryan. "I'll see if I can take a personal day. I don't think it will be a problem with Mrs. Barrett because it will be an educational experience for Ryan."

The doorbell rang, and Max glanced at the clock on the wall. "Parents are arriving. I'll get it."

Max and Tessa sorted the boys' jackets and helped them bundle up as their parents arrived. When they'd all left, Ryan sat in front of the fireplace, zooming a car across the coffee table. Remnants and debris from the party lay scattered from one end of the living room to the other.

Max went to his son and sat on the sofa. "Did you have fun?"

Ryan stopped the car for a moment. "Yeah. I liked Pin the Tail on the Donkey the best."

"That's because you won," Tessa teased as she perched on the hearth. "Wasn't it nice to have friends over?"

Ryan resumed running the car across the table and shrugged.

Tessa exchanged a worried look with Max.

Max picked up a car turned upside down on the floor. "Jimmy liked your room."

Ryan's face lit up. "He says I have *ten* times the cars he does. That's a lot!"

Max was sorry there weren't any children Ryan's age in the immediate neighborhood. "You know, Jimmy only lives about four blocks away. Anytime you want to play with him, I can take you over there or bring Jimmy here. What do you think?"

Ryan shrugged again.

Max ran his hand through his hair. He wished he knew what was going on inside Ryan's head. Maybe he was just tired. It had been a long, exciting day for him. "It's time to put the cars away and get ready for bed."

"Do I hafta get a bath?"

"No. That can wait until tomorrow. Grab as many cars as you can so they don't get lost when we clean up."

Tessa rose from the hearth and stacked paper plates. At the foot of the stairs, Ryan asked over his shoulder, "Are you gonna come up and say good-night?"

Max wondered at Ryan's question. Tessa hadn't missed a night yet. How was his son going to take her leaving?

"I'll be up before you have your pajamas on."

After they tucked Ryan in, Max put the kitchen chairs back where they belonged. He returned to the living room and watched Tessa pluck the papery string confetti from the sofa. One of Ryan's friends had sprayed it a few places other than the prize-winning area.

"I think he had a good time," Max concluded. "He was asleep before we left the room. I just don't get why he doesn't want to be with other kids more."

Tessa dropped the pieces of confetti into her cupped hand then transferred them to the trash can. "I think we should push his friendship with Jimmy. Maybe we can invite him over next week one day after school."

Max gathered soda cups scattered from one end of the room to the other. Each boy must have used three. When Max looked up to see Tessa still working on the sofa, he was struck by the fiery lights of red in her tumbling curls. The flickering flames cast her in a glow. She looked as if she belonged...in his living room, in his life.

She straightened and caught him staring at her. Did her cheeks turn a little rosier? Tessa never blushed, did she?

Grinning at him impishly, she picked up the small aerosol can of string confetti. "Did you have fun tonight?"

"Who had time to think about fun?"

"I bet I know how we can have some fun." The devil danced in her green eyes.

"Uh-oh. I smell trouble."

She tossed him the small can and picked up another. "I challenge you to a duel. Whoever can empty their can on the other person first wins."

"Tessa, I don't know..."

She pressed the button, and orange string confetti shot across Max's chest.

He couldn't believe she was serious. Taking a step toward her, he protested, "Tessa, it will be a mess to clean up."

She winked. "That's why it's fun. Come on, Winthrop. Loosen up." She sprayed the can again, and the string landed on his head and dropped across his face.

"That's it," he growled. "I'll show you how to have fun." In a flash, his thumb pressed the nozzle and strings flew across her head and down her arm. But he didn't let up. He squirted her sweater, her jeans and a dangling string landed on her nose.

But Tessa was quick. Darting away from him, she danced around the sofa. He chased, and she squirted. She got his hand. "Score another one for me!"

He shook his can. "But mine's almost empty. And look at you."

She didn't fall for the bait but launched another attack until he sprayed her again and most of it stuck to her sweater. "No fair," she protested. "Your arms are longer."

He chuckled. "I guess you'll have to be inventive to compensate."

Wrinkling her nose at him, she jumped up on the sofa for a better aim. Max couldn't let her get the upper hand. Scooping her up in his arms, he plopped her on the sofa before she realized his intention. She clambered to her knees, sputtering, "You—you—caveman!" She squirted the confetti.

Max sprayed her back, both of them attacking nonstop until they were laughing and out of breath. Lodging one knee on the sofa, he leaned toward her for one last winning spurt. Suddenly he didn't care about winning the game. Tessa's face glowed; her lips were pink from pursing them in concentration. Her cheeks were rosy from their game and the warmth of the fire. She looked absolutely silly wreathed in orange confetti, but so lovely.

His laughter was a rumble in his chest when she stopped giggling. They seemed locked in place for an eternal moment, then inexorably drawn together. He gathered her in his arms and pulled her toward him. She was warmth and loveliness, softness and adventure, fun and passion. Friendship could never describe the desire roaring through his blood with only one destination. Lifting her onto his lap, he kissed her with the fervor he'd denied, the wanting he'd tried to ignore, the need that had built up for too long.

He didn't wait for her to open her lips, but pushed inside. Her small moan told him he'd done the right thing. And as she welcomed his probing tongue, he knew she wanted him as much as he wanted her. He was familiar with needing and wanting. He just wasn't used to having the sensations satisfied. Tessa gave as much as he did, took as much as he did.

Still, he wanted more. Tasting her secrets wasn't enough. He wanted to touch them, too. The hem of her sweater stretched easily, giving him access. The skin of her midriff was hot, satiny, inviting. As he ran his fingers across it slowly, she moved against his hand as if she wanted more, too. His fingertips slid along the edge of her bra. It was silky and wispy and not at all what he'd expected. Tessa was so self-reliant, so strong. But so feminine, too. He shouldn't be surprised. That's what he loved about Tessa; she constantly surprised him.

Loved? No, it couldn't be. He loved Leslie. Didn't he? This passion for Tessa was just that, wasn't it? Passion mixed with caring.

Tessa felt Max's hand on her breast. The silky material was thin, but not thin enough. She wanted to feel the ridge of his fingers, the heat of his palm. He was kissing her as if he never wanted to stop. And she didn't want him to stop. He'd lit a fire in her heart, her soul, her body. She loved his arms around her, she loved his lips on hers, she loved his scent, his texture, his consummate maleness. She loved him.

The shock of the realization made her go still. Loved Max? Everything inside her cried, *No! That can't happen.* But it had. She knew the truth when she saw it, heard it, felt it.

He must have sensed the change in her, the reversal from passion to panic. Her stomach felt queasy; her heart pounded in her ears.

His hand left her skin and he pulled away.

She was afraid to look at him for fear he'd see the truth in her eyes, on her face. Wishing the corner of the sofa was in her flat in London and she could be there with a blink of her eyes, she slid from his lap as gracefully as she could. She couldn't face him now; she simply couldn't.

Max was silent, and the silence was worse than denials and excuses. He thought their passion was wrong. He didn't have to say it. She knew.

The orange string confetti sticking all over her sweater reminded Tessa of her foolishness.

"We have a mess to clean up," Max said in a low tone, his voice husky.

He shifted on the sofa, and Tessa realized how uncomfortable he must be. "Max, you don't have to say anything. I know you haven't dated since Leslie died and the pressure builds up—"

He swore, a fiery, succinct epithet. "I'm not a balloon ready to pop!"

She curled up tighter, swinging her legs underneath her. "Max, think about it. This close proximity, the old feelings we shared . . ."

"I don't have to think about it," he snapped. "I have to deal with it."

"And you think I don't?"

He rubbed the back of his neck. "I suppose the situation is hard for you, too. Neither of us expected . . ." He inhaled a deep breath. "We only have a few more weeks. Do you know when you're leaving?"

"November seventeenth."

He went silent again.

There didn't seem to be anything else to say. Even if there had been, Tessa couldn't sit still another minute. Too much was going on inside her. And she wanted to escape it all. Hopping up, she plucked a long string of confetti from the sofa arm. Moving quickly, she cleaned off the back while Max watched.

Finally he pushed himself up. His face was still and set, the nerve on his jaw working. "This could wait until tomorrow."

She had to get them back on a comfortable footing or she'd never get through the next few weeks. "Never put off till tomorrow what you can do today."

He didn't even grimace at the old proverb. Rather, he picked up the cups that had landed on the hearth when they'd begun their confetti battle. With an "I'll load the dishwasher," he strode into the kitchen.

Tessa sighed with relief. She needed time to be alone. She needed time to think. Maybe she could think her feelings into a semblance of order. She fervently hoped so.

* * *

Tessa sat on the bed in her room Monday evening, typing notes into her computer on the practicality of Americans buying property overseas. Her fingers didn't fly over the keys as they usually did. Nor did she organize in her head as she went along. Tonight organization seemed impossible. She typed words, statistics, phrases, but the information wasn't jelling.

Since Saturday night, Tessa had thought about loving Max, she'd feared loving Max, she'd resented the panic that overtook her each time the feelings welled up. She'd tried not to act differently around him. But knowing she loved him changed everything. Except her life. She was a foreign correspondent with a good record, a reliable reputation, a bright future. But most of all, she had no indication Max felt anything but desire, desire he obviously didn't want to feel.

On Sunday, they'd taken Ryan roller-skating again. And they'd avoided each other. Tonight, Max had driven Ryan to his Cub Scout meeting and had said he'd run errands before picking up Ryan to come home. It was obvious he didn't want to be alone with her. Did she want to be alone with him? Knowing what could happen?

Thinking about it brought heat to her cheeks.

She heard the back door open and before she could even think about shutting down her computer, Ryan pounded up the stairs and burst into her room.

Max's voice boomed from the stairway. "Knock first, Ryan."

It was already too late for that.

"Sorry," Ryan mumbled.

She smiled and waved him toward the bed. "That's okay. How was your meeting?"

"Fine." He shifted back and forth on his feet and played with the yellow tie of his uniform.

"What did you do?"

"Made a Halloween mask. It's downstairs."

Max stood in the doorway, one hand high on the doorjamb. His jeans were snug and showed wear at the knees. He wore no belt and the waistband rode low on his hips. His red-and-black flannel shirt clothed his upper torso with rugged, lumberjack appeal. His gaze as it found and held hers was as neutral as his expression. He'd make a terrific poker player.

Ryan came closer to the bed.

Max said softly, "Go ahead and ask her."

Ryan looked terribly uncertain. Tessa set her computer on the bed and slid to the edge, dropping her legs over the side. She patted the spread beside her. "Come here and tell me what's going on."

Ryan glanced at Max, then crawled up beside her. "We're havin' somethin' special at school."

"It's a pageant," Max explained. "Ryan didn't tell me until tonight that he has a special part."

"I'm gonna be a Pilgrim!" he declared proudly. "It's about the first Thanksgiving. Dad always comes to watch. Can you come, too?"

Tessa thought about going into the school again, seeing all the families together, the hordes of kids, the noise and chatter that had always resoundingly reminded her that she didn't fit in, that she didn't have a family to care whether or not she took a part in a play, or a concert, or a pageant. She shivered as old memories haunted her. A half-hour meeting with Mrs. Barrett was one thing. A few hours smack dab in the middle of all the commotion was another.

There was something else to think about, too. She and Max and Ryan *weren't* a family. She was becoming more and more attached to Ryan. How did he feel about her? The more she did things with him and for him, the harder it would be for him when she left.

Max was watching her closely.

"Ryan, I don't know. What with leaving for New York this weekend, I'm going to be pretty busy."

"But you're not leavin' till Friday!" His lip quivered. "And the pageant's Thursday night."

She felt awful. She wanted to give him everything she could. But the truth was—she *would* be leaving. She'd been entirely available to Ryan and Max since she'd arrived in Jenkins. Maybe that had been a monumental mistake—for all of them.

"Honey, I need to think about it, okay?"

His face fell with disappointment and he looked to his father for encouragement.

Max straightened and filled the doorway. "Let Tessa think about it, slugger. You go get your pajamas on. We'll talk about it again tomorrow."

Ryan's tone was somber. "Okay." He turned back to Tessa. "I really want you to come."

Tessa's breath caught in her chest. What was the right thing to do? Right for Max and her and Ryan.

Ryan slipped by his father and went to his room.

Tessa expected Max to leave, too. But he didn't. Instead, he stepped closer to the bed, his forehead creased, his scowl manifesting his anger. "*How* could you do that to him?"

Chapter Eight

Tessa felt guilty enough. "I'm not doing anything to him, Max."

Max advanced on her, his eyes a deepening, intimidating brown. "He wants you to be there."

Squaring her shoulders and tilting her chin, a response gathered force and exploded. "And I wanted *my* mother to be there, too!"

He looked taken aback for a moment. "So you want Ryan to suffer as you did?"

Damn! Max had the power to rattle her the way no one else could. "I'm *not* Ryan's mother. And it's not good for him to pretend I am."

Max cocked his head and studied her for a moment. "You think that's what he's doing?"

All the defensiveness she'd felt when Max attacked her deflated and she was left with confusion. "I don't know. But if he is, it's got to stop. I won't be helping him, I'll be hurting him. Maybe I've hurt him already."

Where Max's advance before had been quick and angry, it was now slow and cautious. "You can't believe loving him is hurting him."

"I'm saying his depending on me might be."

Max eyed her curiously. "What else is going on, Tessa?"

"I don't know what you mean." She lowered her head a fraction so she wasn't meeting his probing regard. Sliding around on the bed, she shuffled her notes into a neat pile.

"You're a lousy liar." Max rubbed his chin thoughtfully. "You were jittery when we talked to Mrs. Barrett. You couldn't sit still or get out of that school fast enough. Was school difficult for you?"

He was stabbing in the dark. But she knew how unremittingly persistent Max could be. "We all have rough years."

He wouldn't accept the generality. Before she could take a breath, he stood beside the bed...beside her. "Which year was rough for you? Second grade, like Ryan? Third? Seventh?"

The papers on the bed next to her became all important. "I'd rather not discuss it."

His large, warm hand came down on her shoulder. "Look at me, Tessa." When she didn't, he said gently, "You have to stop running from things you don't want to see."

Now she looked at him, filled with anger and resentment and pain. "What do you know about it? Why do you think you know how I should live my life?"

He crouched down in front of her, much as he would with Ryan. "What don't I know? Tell me."

Suddenly she was swept back into being a six-year-old again, sitting in that echoing hallway while the principal tried to call her mother—the mother she'd never see again. Her hands trembled and she closed them into fists.

Max covered both of her hands with one of his. "Tessa?"

The gentleness and caring in his voice undid her. "My mother left me at the school. She dropped me off in the morning and she never came back." Tessa wouldn't open her eyes because she didn't want to see Max's pity. She didn't need pity; she never had.

Stroking her hair away from her forehead, Max pushed it behind her ear. "And the rest of your school life reminded you of that day."

She nodded and swallowed the lump in her throat. "Until college. Everything was new there. I felt I could really start to be somebody important, not different. My profs accepted me for who I was, not what I came from."

"You *are* somebody important, somebody special."

Her eyes grew moist. More than anything she wanted to burrow into Max's arms and let him hold her. But they were too volatile together now. "I don't want to hurt Ryan."

Max's hand kept comforting, stroking, soothing. "Then tell him the truth."

She reared back away from his touch. "About my mother?"

Ryan called from his room, "Dad, Tessa. I'm ready."

Max rose to his feet. "It'll help him understand if you decide not to go."

Tessa started practicing what she'd say in her head because she knew Max was right.

* * *

The Pilgrims stood on one side of the long table on the stage, the Native Americans on the other. Ryan, as leader for the Pilgrims, crossed to the chief and extended his hand in friendship.

Max's arm nudged Tessa's shoulder, and she could feel him leaning forward to watch more intently. He made her feel safe and protected sitting here, and for a good part of the last hour, memories had washed over her not causing their usual pain.

Tessa had briefly explained to Ryan about her mother leaving her in a school and not coming back. She'd told him how she felt unhappy and sad whenever she entered a school. His eyes had grown huge and round, and she'd thought she'd seen questions there. But he didn't ask any. He'd said quietly, "You don't have to come if it makes you feel bad." It was as if he understood with the wisdom of someone much older. Then and there she'd decided going to his pageant was the best thing she could do for him to show him that her love for him could overcome the past hurts.

And it had.

She gazed around again at the audience in the auditorium. Mothers, fathers, brothers and sisters. People she'd longed for in her life. Yet, seeing the families together now didn't hurt so much. Tessa watched a toddler two rows in front of her as the child laid her head on her mother's shoulder and popped her thumb into her mouth.

Tessa had never thought about having children. Her own childhood had been so unhappy. And she'd dismissed marriage. With her career, it would be impossible, wouldn't it? Yet the past few weeks, living with Max, taking care of Ryan, she could almost envision it.

As the Pilgrims and Native Americans shared a feast on the stage, Tessa realized Ryan loved her unconditionally. She also realized something else that made her shake in her shoes. She'd love to be his mother. More and more, she felt as if she belonged here. Could loving Max assuage the feeling of apartness she'd always experienced? Dare she love Max when he'd belonged to Leslie? Did he feel anything for her besides physical attraction? Sometimes he was so understanding, so gentle. . . . But then, that was Max. He'd act that way toward any woman.

Exactly what was she contemplating? Changing the life she led? Didn't she want to travel? Fly to exciting new places? Did she dare think about a life with Max?

Thank God, she was going to New York this weekend. Maybe she could get some perspective away from here.

Friday evening, Max and Ryan gazed inside the glass and chrome jewelry case in the New Haven department store. Max remembered the chain around Tessa's neck when she'd shown him her mother's ring. It had looked old and worn. The chain he spotted inside this case was shiny, fourteen carat and sparkling as it caught and reflected the light.

"When are we gonna give Tessa her presents?" Ryan asked as he pressed his nose up against the glass case.

"When she gets back on Sunday."

Ryan's hands joined his nose on the glass. "I miss her."

Max couldn't believe how much he did, too. He'd picked up Ryan at the sitter's and they'd come home to an empty house. It was an odd feeling. For the past month, Tessa had been there every day. Some days she was cooking, some days on the phone, some days typing on her computer. But she'd always been there.

"Dad, Tessa's gonna have her birthday alone."

"When she gets back, we can have a cake."

"But her birthday's tomorrow. She'll be all alone."

The idea didn't sit well with Max, either, especially after Tessa's latest revelation about her childhood. He crouched down beside Ryan as he always did when he wanted to talk to his son about something important. "What do you think about me going to New York and keeping Tessa company?"

Ryan forgot the jewelry in the case and turned toward Max.

"I can't go?"

"New York is mostly for grown-ups. But they do have a museum with dinosaur bones. Maybe another weekend you and I could go look at them."

Ryan scrubbed the toe of his sneaker against the tile floor. "What are you and Tessa gonna do?"

"Probably get all dressed up and go to dinner."

Ryan wrinkled his nose in distaste. Then he asked, "New York's not very far away, is it?"

"Only about two hours."

Ryan thought about it. "I think you oughta go and make sure..."

"What?"

Ryan ducked his chin. "Nothin'."

"Ryan, you're sure it's okay with you if I go?"

"Can Emma and Scruffy come over?"

"We can ask."

Ryan took a few moments to decide. "Yeah, you go and bring Tessa home soon."

Max could feel the warmth of Tessa's leg as the cab swerved around a corner. The taxi driver honked his horn at the car double-parked in front of him. With another honk and a screech of wheels, he veered around the vehicle. Tessa's hip bumped Max's as she slid against him on the cracked vinyl seat.

Max didn't mind and he didn't move away. He wondered if her beige coat was new. It wasn't easily packable like her trench coat. And the dress underneath—

The royal blue dress with its low V neck, short puffed sleeves and slim, short skirt brought out the sleek lines and tempting curves Tessa usually hid underneath jeans and a sweatshirt. She wasn't hiding anything tonight.

When he'd called Tessa, she'd seemed happy to hear from him, though definitely surprised. Regretfully she'd told him she'd made plans to meet friends for a late dinner. So he'd asked her to go to the theater instead. She'd said she'd love to go with him, and he was welcome to come along for dinner. Somehow she'd managed to get tickets for a hot show on Broadway. He hadn't minded sitting toward the back of the theater, because he hadn't cared about the show. He only cared about being with Tessa. As the taxi wove in and out of traffic toward the restaurant, he wondered if Dan Holloway would be there.

Like many restaurants in New York, Henry's didn't look like much on the outside. But as soon as Max stepped inside, he could feel the understated elegance. It was dimly lit by gleaming brass chandeliers. Wrought-iron partitions afforded diners a modicum of privacy. Rose linens trimmed in black set off the sparkling crystal goblets and spotless silverware. After Max checked Tessa's coat, they walked up to the maître d' at his little black podium.

"Ms. Kahill. It's good to see you again. Your friends have already arrived. I've placed you at the back round table."

"Thank you," she said with a bright smile as she followed the tuxedoed man to the rear of the restaurant.

Max had often wondered about Tessa's world. Now he was glimpsing it.

A woman and three men sat at the round table. They were involved in lively conversation, but it stopped when Max and Tessa reached the table. One of the men whistled, another pretended to wipe his brow as his gaze ran up and down Tessa's dress, the third just smiled.

The woman gave them all a "down-boys" glare. "Ignore them. They've been on assignment too long."

"After that trek into the rain forest, Tessa looks mighty good. Of course, so do you, Louise."

The petite brunette laughed. "Still a master at tact, Dan." She turned to Tessa. "How are you? It's been awhile."

Tessa nodded. "Orly. Last year."

"I hear you're covering the Summit," Louise commented. "Lucky girl."

Max nodded to the maître d' that he would seat Tessa. As he pulled her chair out for her, she said, "Before we start talking shop, I want everyone to meet Max Winthrop."

The men shook his hand. Louise smiled. As he seated Tessa and took the chair beside her, he examined Dan Holloway more closely. Mid-forties. Thick but graying hair. Blue eyes that seemed to concentrate on Tessa much too long. Unfortunately he was sitting across from her so he had a good view. But Max was close enough to touch her. His body responded to the thought.

Tessa spread her napkin on her lap. "Have you ordered yet?"

"Just drinks," Louise answered. She addressed Max. "How do you know Tessa? Are you in TV? Print?"

Max glanced at Tessa, not knowing how much she'd told any of these people. "We've known each other for years. I came to New York to help her celebrate—" A sharp kick to his shin made him turn in her direction. She was smiling sweetly, but he got the message. "To help her celebrate her upcoming trip to Oslo."

"Prime assignment," the man introduced as Joe muttered. "First time Williamson put a woman on something like that."

Louise jabbed his arm. "This is the nineties."

Holloway gibed, "Is that why your most-publicized piece was about the fall fashion line?"

"Okay, so we don't all get the plums," Louise admitted with a wry shake of her head. "I'm just glad Tessa has climbed the ladder and hasn't hit the glass ceiling. She'll make it easier for me to climb."

It was obvious that Tessa's colleagues respected her. And it was even more obvious during conversation over dinner that Tessa and the others spoke their own language and were much more knowledgeable about the world's affairs than Max was.

By the time dessert arrived, Louise poured cream into her coffee and said, "Enough about politics. Don't we have anything else to talk about?"

The others around the table looked at each other, were silent a moment, then broke into smiles. Tessa laughed. "I guess not." She looked at Max. "You must be bored to death."

His eyes connected with and held hers. "No. Fascinated, actually. Do you realize all of you are part of history in the making?" He nodded to Joe. "You being present when the Berlin wall fell." He gestured to Dan. "Making environmental concerns an issue." Covering Tessa's hand with his on the table, he instantly felt a heat that was more than skin touching skin. He remembered what he'd been about to say. "You'll be recording what will happen at the Summit. Do you feel as if you're part of history when you're doing it?"

Joe shrugged. "I guess we're too close to each event to see the sum total. What do you do, Max?"

"I teach high-school math and try to make it applicable to kids' lives when I can."

Louise's lips puckered in a small O. "Now that's a job I wouldn't want. I don't see how you can deal with teenagers day after day. You must have a ton of patience."

"And I don't see how you travel constantly, remember what city you're in and don't have constant jet lag," Max returned.

Dan responded, "Every job has its trade-offs. I guess it all boils down to what you like to do and what you want out of life. My camera keeps me seeing the world differently every day." He grinned. "The excitement ain't bad, either."

Quiet descended on the table, and Louise and Joe agreed with secret smiles that said they shared Dan's view. Max surveyed Tessa, but she just looked pensive as she took another bite of cheesecake.

Music began playing on the other side of the restaurant. It was easy and slow, and Max suddenly wanted Tessa in his arms. He leaned closer to her and the elusive fragrance of her perfume teased him. "Would you like to dance?"

Transferring her napkin from her lap to the table, she answered, "Yes, I would."

They excused themselves, and Max kept a protective hand on her back as they wove around the partitions and tables. The fabric of her dress was smooth and slippery under his fingers. Once on the small wooden dance floor, Max took Tessa in his arms, her right hand in his, her left resting close to his neck. The tantalizing but discreet contact made his heart beat faster. "I hope I'm not cramping your style. If you'd rather be back there talking about your work..."

"I talk about work every time I see them. I've never danced with you before."

"Sure, you have. Two weeks ago."

"That wasn't quite like this."

As he pulled Tessa slightly closer, strictly for comfort's sake, of course, he had to agree. That had been nothing like this. "Why didn't you want them to know it's your birthday?"

Her shoulders lifted and fell, making the material slide under his hand. "I don't like a fuss. Besides," she teased, "a woman my age soon stops counting."

He chuckled. "A woman your age? Did you add on a few years that I don't know about?"

A lingering smile turned up her lips. "Only that day I finished Ryan's lopsided costume and grew a few gray hairs."

Max played with the curls on the nape of her neck. "I can't thank you enough for helping Ryan the way you have."

The pulse at her throat fluttered in rhythm with his. "We still don't know what's bothering him."

If Max kept touching her hair, kept looking at her perfectly curved mouth, he'd have to kiss her. "Maybe it will work itself out," he said gruffly.

"I don't know, Max. Childhood problems don't just disappear. They carry over no matter how old you get."

Max guided Tessa in silence for a few moments. "I worry about Ryan being an only child. There are inherent problems in that. He doesn't have to share. He gets all my attention. And I wonder if he's lonely."

"He doesn't have to be an only child forever. You could remarry." The slight tilt of her head, the quirk of her brows, seemed questioning though she'd uttered a statement.

It was on the tip of Max's tongue to ask if she was applying for the job. But he realized he couldn't ask in a teasing way because her answer would have too much significance. "Yes, I guess I could."

She seemed startled by his reply. Her green eyes grew as dark as an evening forest and just as mysterious. Would she ever think about settling down? He couldn't imagine her ditching her career. It meant too much to her. A nagging voice inside his head whispered, *She stayed to help Ryan.* But he couldn't listen to the voice and take any comfort from it because her staying was strictly short-term.

As other couples crowded the dance floor, Max tightened his arm around Tessa and brought her hand to his chest. The sensation of her softness against him went straight to his head and other more elemental parts of his body. The burning realization that he wanted more than to simply be pressed against her made him finally face up to the facts. He wanted to take Tessa to bed. He wanted to make love to her, hold her throughout the night and wake up with her in the morning. Did that mean he was ready to put his marriage to Leslie in the past? Did that mean he wanted an affair with Tessa? Because that's all he could ever have.

Tessa succumbed to the delicious tingling that had begun as soon as Max surrounded her with his arms. She told herself this was simply one dance, nothing more. But the feel of his wool suit coat against her cheek, his arm possessively holding her, his fingers intertwined with hers, led her to believe this was where she wanted to stay for longer than one dance.

If she lifted her head just a smidgen, her lips would brush his jaw. She imagined pressing them there, whispering . . . I love you? What could that mean for them? Max was as traditional as ever. Time hadn't changed that. Even if she'd find a job in New York, could he accept a working wife? *Whoa, girl. Reality check. You have no idea what Max feels.*

As he closed her more tightly in his arms and his lower body pressed against hers, she did know he desired her. She thought he'd back away, but he didn't. Swaying with her, guiding their small steps, it seemed he needed to just feel and enjoy the desire and closeness, too.

After another dance and another hour of conversation with Tessa's cohorts, Max and Tessa caught a cab and went back to the hotel. Max asked Tessa to wait at the elevator while he stopped at the desk. She covered her mouth with her hand to stifle a yawn, not thinking much about it.

When he joined her and they stepped into the elevator, he only pushed the button for her floor. "I'll walk you to your room."

Before this stay with Max, she might have protested. Before this stay with Max, he never would have joined her in New York. Everything had shifted and changed between them.

At her door, he took a package from his pocket. It was a small rectangular box wrapped in silver paper with a tiny white bow. "Ryan has something to give you when you get back. I'd rather give this to you now. Happy Birthday, Tessa."

Her fingers trembled as she unwrapped the box. She did it slowly, stalling, prolonging the moment. She'd received few gifts in her life. Leslie had always remembered her birthday. But this... this gift she'd remember forever. "Are you sure Ryan was all right with you coming to New York?"

"He was fine with it. He wanted me to come to make sure you came back to Jenkins."

An alarm went off inside Tessa. Was Ryan afraid she'd leave him as Leslie had? Lord knows, she was becoming more and more sure she didn't want to leave....

Max took the paper from her fingers and stuffed it into his pocket. She stared at the box, almost afraid to lift the lid.

"Open it," he urged gently.

Nestled on a soft bed of cotton, she found a sparkling gold chain. Her hand shook as she gently slid her finger under it, bringing it from the box. "Oh, Max. It's beautiful."

"I noticed the one holding your ring looked worn. The salesclerk said this would be strong enough to hold it, plus it's something called diamond cut so you can wear it alone."

Tessa's eyes misted over at Max's thoughtfulness. To do something like this... didn't that prove he cared? "Will you put it on for me?"

He smiled a slow, lazy smile that made her pulse leap. "Isn't it a little late? In a few minutes you'll be getting undressed."

That thought created pictures that made her shake because she thought of him undressed, waiting in bed for her.... Holding the chain out to him, she turned around, not able to find a suitable reply. She wanted to feel the gold next to her skin; she wanted to see it gleam; she never wanted to take it off.

Max clasped it, then lifted her hair to let the necklace slide properly in place. The pads of his thumbs along her nape, his tall presence behind her, his caring, caused her breath to come in short puffs.

Gently, he turned her around. Gazing into her eyes, he said, "Beautiful."

She leaned closer to him, wanting an intimacy that scared her to death because she'd never wanted it before—not like this. He bent to her. Their lips touched and clung. The kiss was so tender that a longing and yearning and aching greater than Tessa had ever known swept through her. Breathless from the impact, she parted her lips.

Max caressed the small of her back, bringing her slightly closer. Everything about Max excited her, intensified the desires that had lain dormant for so long. He was stability and comfort and safety, but passion and adventure, too. And she loved him. Irrevocably.

Max gauged his response, called on his self-discipline and restraint as his tongue glided against hers. He'd known her kiss would arouse him easily, just as dancing close to her had. But tonight he'd wanted to steal whatever he could get without going too far. Now he was at his limit. Why couldn't Tessa want the same things from life he did? Why couldn't she be...more like Leslie? No. Then she wouldn't be Tessa.

He slowly ended the kiss, wishing, hoping, dreaming. But when he opened his eyes, he had to face reality—Tessa standing at a hotel-room door. Tessa's life.

Her cheeks were rosy, her mouth shiny from his kiss. Clearing her throat, she reverently touched the necklace. "Would you like to come in?" She quickly added, "We could call room service and order coffee...or something."

If he stepped into that room, they'd both regret it in the morning. "It's late. I'd better not."

Her fingers hadn't left the chain. "Thank you, Max."

All the sensations rushing through him were bittersweet, both enjoyable and painful. "You're welcome. Do you have your key?"

Taking it from her purse, she slid the card into the lock. The green light flickered, and she opened the door. "Good night, Max."

"Good night, birthday girl. Sleep well."

Her shy smile, her just-kissed expression, the longing in her eyes, almost led him to throw caution and reality to the wind by hauling her into his arms again and carrying her to the bed. But his conscience and his discipline took him a step back.

Tessa went inside and let the door close behind her.

Dancing in New York was but a dream as Tessa sat on one of the sets at WHBT, waiting for the camera to roll. Since this was a live show, the host, Mark Thompson, watched the monitor, waiting for his cue after a briefing of news and weather.

Tessa hadn't met Mark before this morning, but he seemed personable enough and eagerly interested in her career. They'd had a brief discussion about her past experiences and the upcoming Summit, and he'd told her he'd stick to those topics.

Tessa smoothed her skirt over her knees. The dress she'd worn to the school dance had seemed appropriate. Because of the flared skirt she wouldn't have to worry about too much leg showing. Not particularly nervous about the interview, she *was* nervous about Max sitting in the audience watching. Ever since they'd returned from New York, his regard had been penetrating, his silences disturbing. Even as she'd blown out her candles on the birthday cake Ryan and Emma had baked for her, his gaze hadn't missed a pucker of her lips or the tears that had collected in her eyes as the familial feeling of belonging overwhelmed her.

One of the cameramen gave her the signal they'd be "on" in ten seconds. She took a deep breath.

Smiling, Mark introduced Tessa, then led her through a brief résumé of her career, from her first job in New York to the break when a fellow correspondent had gotten the flu and Tessa had been sent overseas to cover a government coup in his place. Using her wits and daring, she'd discovered where the deposed leader had been hiding and obtained an exclusive interview. Her free-lance career had been launched and her articles demanded attention.

As the station broke for a commercial, Tessa's gaze met Max's. His frown cut deep into his cheeks. Because of his attitude about her life-style, she'd never told him much about her career. She supposed he was hearing a lot of this for the first time. Evidently he didn't approve. A deep sadness filled Tessa's heart. If Max couldn't accept who she'd been, who she was now, they'd never have a chance at a . . .

Readjusting his microphone, Mark Thompson looked on cue into the main camera and reintroduced Tessa and the segment. But this time instead of proceeding to the subject of the Summit as Tessa expected, he took an entirely different tack.

Facing her more squarely, he asked, "So what do you see yourself doing ten years from now?"

She kept from glancing toward Max. "I don't plan that far ahead."

Thompson smiled again disarmingly. "Give it a shot."

With a small shrug, she said, "I love my work. I wouldn't have taken the chances I have or traveled so much if I didn't. Even when I'm sixty, I hope I'll still be involved in this business somehow."

The host shifted in his chair, obviously not expecting her to be so vague. "I imagine your career makes a personal life difficult."

"It does." She didn't elaborate.

"Have you managed close relationships? Exciting affairs? Cross-country romances?"

Tessa thought about Ryan sitting in the audience and could have slugged Thompson gladly. But that would only increase his ratings. "People outside of my profession like to glamorize it. I do my job. Whatever happens along the way, happens." Tessa was aware of Max in the audience. His scowl. His tense posture. Was he perturbed with her or Thompson?

"But, Ms. Kahill, I'm sure the viewers want to know exactly how your profession affects your personal life."

Hoping to throw him off guard, she retorted, "Inquiring minds want to know?"

He accepted the gibe and grinned. "Of course, they do. Tell us about at least one of your experiences. It would be something for a young reporter to think about if he or she were considering doing what you do.''

She'd give Thompson what he wanted and hopefully he'd move on. "Once I met another journalist in a foreign country under siege. We turned to each other when the going got dangerous. I thought I'd found someone who could share the excitement and the travel. He thought . . ." She sighed. It didn't hurt anymore but reminded her how naive she'd been. "He didn't care about sharing his life, just the six weeks while he was there."

"So are you saying to have a career like yours, a woman would have to put her personal life on hold?"

She took a deep breath and exhaled slowly. "That's for each individual to decide. My career is important to me. To have a relationship, I'd need someone special in my life who could understand that and give me the freedom I need."

Her serious, honest answers stopped Thompson from probing any further. He went to commercial.

Chapter Nine

Max didn't say much as he and Tessa and Ryan toured the television station. Tessa didn't like this silence between them, the uncertainty it caused. But she also knew from experience that Max would tell her what was on his mind when he was ready.

They stopped at a fast-food restaurant for lunch where Ryan chattered about everything he'd seen at the television station. When they got back to the house, Tessa was halfway up the steps with the intention of changing her clothes when Max came to the foot of the stairs and said, "There's a message on the machine for you." His expression was remote, his tone even and controlled. But the nerve on his jaw worked.

"I'll get it when I come down."

His voice level didn't change. "You might want to get it now."

To give her room to pass, he moved away from the bottom step. Not grazing his tall body, not touching him, created as much excitement and awareness as if she had. Going to the machine in the living room, she pressed the Play button.

"Tessa, it's Dan. Brushfires in California are out of control. I'm flying out tonight and I want you with me. *News of the Week* committed. They'll spring for you to go, too. Don't let me down on this, Tessa. Our flight leaves at eight. We'll be gone four days tops, I promise. Give me a call ASAP." He rattled off a number.

"I think you should go."

Tessa swung around. "What?"

Max stuffed his hands into the pockets of his khaki slacks. "You want to go, I know you do. You missed Brazil. You've given me and Ryan six weeks. We can't expect you to put your life or your career on hold."

He was saying all the right words, but something about them didn't ring true. "What about Ryan?"

A glittering hardness entered Max's eyes that allowed no glimpse into his emotions. "You'll be leaving in two weeks, anyway. He might as well deal with it now."

She dragged her hand across her forehead. "I don't know, Max."

"It's best for everyone if you go. All our lives have to get back to normal."

If Max didn't want her here, if he thought this would be best for Ryan... She could use some time away to consider what *she* wanted, too. Before she had the opportunity to think about it any longer, Max decided, "I'll go tell Ryan. You call Holloway."

"Maybe I should tell Ryan."

Max pulled his hands from his pockets and strode to the stairs without even looking over his shoulder. "If you have time, you can talk to him, but I imagine you'll have to be off to New York." And with that he climbed to the second floor.

What was wrong with Max? What had she said that had made him so...distant? Or had he finally realized she had a career and she'd never be the type of woman he wanted, the type of woman Leslie had been?

Tessa's suitcase stood ready by the door. A weight much heavier than that suitcase lay on Max's chest. Brushfires. Why the hell had he encouraged her to go?

Because she'd wanted to go. He'd seen it in her eyes. Tessa's wanderlust couldn't be cured by him or anyone else. Her TV interview had made that abundantly clear. She wanted freedom. What kind of relationship could two people have if one of them was always traipsing off to God knew where? Let alone raise a child, or children. Watching Ryan now with his wide, questioning brown eyes, Max suspected his son was as unsettled by this trip of Tessa's as he was. But they both had to get used to the idea that nothing about Tessa was permanent.

Tessa came down the stairs looking uncertain, her trench coat hung over her arm. Ryan sat on the sofa next to Max, quietly fidgeting with his fingers. Even when he heard Tessa, he didn't move.

She crossed to the sofa and knelt beside him, kissing his forehead. "I'll only be gone a few days."

He looked up at her with quiet, sad eyes and didn't say anything.

Tessa rose to her feet.

Max pushed himself up. "I'll walk you to the car."

As soon as they stepped outside, she laid her hand on his arm. "Max, maybe I shouldn't go."

Her hand on his arm felt too good, too right. "What good will that do? You'll be leaving for the Summit. Eventually he has to accept the fact that you're not staying."

"But maybe we didn't prepare him enough. Maybe this was too quick—"

The front door pushed open, and Ryan came tumbling out. "Tessa, Tessa. What did I do wrong? Please don't go away." Tears ran down his cheeks unchecked.

Max's heart twisted and he lifted Ryan into his arms. "You didn't do anything wrong. Why would you think that?" When Ryan ducked his head and wouldn't answer, Max looked at Tessa. All the color had drained from her face. Holding Ryan in one arm, Max cupped her elbow. "Tessa?"

Tessa tried to absorb the full impact of Ryan's question. Bits of conversation she'd had with him fell into place. Her own unresolved hurts from childhood flooded in and she suddenly understood exactly what was bothering Ryan, what had been bothering him for a long time.

She dragged up her voice. "Let's go inside."

"But you'll miss your plane...."

"Let's go inside," she repeated.

Once in the house, she sank down on the second step of the stairway and held out her arms to Ryan. "Come here, honey."

Max put him down, and Ryan didn't hesitate to come to her. She patted the step next to her, and he sat. Curving her arm around his shoulders, she asked, "Do you know why your mom died?"

Max's brows arched and he looked as if he was going to protest when Ryan said, "She got sick and went to the hospital and never came back. When I get sick and go to the doctor's, I come back home!''

Tessa's arm tightened around his shoulders. "Your mom got a kind of sickness that doesn't get better. She wanted to come home, honey, honest she did.'' Tessa's voice caught. ''Because she loved you so much. But the sickness made her weak and tired and it took her away. Her dying had nothing to do with you. If she could have come home and been your mom forever, she would have.''

Ryan focused on one point. "She still loved me? Even after she went away?'' he asked, his gaze and voice hopeful.

''Yes, she did. And she still loves you now. Mommies love their children forever, even if they have to go away.'' Tessa squeezed his shoulder. ''You did nothing wrong. Her getting sick, her not coming home, had nothing to do with you. It was just an awful thing that happened.''

Ryan looked down at the strings of his sneakers. "But one of the kids at school, his dad left and didn't come back. Brian said it's because he was bad and his mom and dad yelled about him all the time . . . and I thought I did something to make my mommy go away. . . .''

Tessa laid her head against Ryan's and hugged him tighter. "You are the best little boy anybody could want. Sometimes things happen and we can't do anything about them.''

Max crouched down in front of Ryan. "What did you think you did wrong?''

Ryan shrugged. "I thought and thought and thought. But I don't 'member Mommy very much.''

Tessa lifted Ryan's chin. "Ryan, if I tell you I'm going to come back, will you believe me?''

He glanced away into the living room. Then he faced her again. "Can you promise?"

Feeling her heart lift a little, she smiled. "Yes, I can promise. And I can call you from California. I can't promise to call every night, because I might not be near a phone, but I can call you when I get there and I can call you before I come home. If I can call in between, I will. Do you believe me?"

He hesitated, then nodded.

"Good. And I'd like you to do something for me. Everyday I'm gone, you draw me a picture of something you did and you can tell me all about it when I get back. Okay?"

Ryan's grin spread from one side of his face to the other.

Max brushed Ryan's hair from his forehead. "We love you, Ryan. No matter what you do or what you say or how old you get, we'll always love you." Max gave his son a hug, and Tessa brushed a lone tear from her cheek.

Ryan hopped up and ordered, "Don't leave 'til I come back. I wanna get something." Turning, he ran up the stairs.

Tessa said to Max in a low voice, "I should have known."

He frowned. "How could you know?"

Her eyes lifted slowly to his as the pain rose up and spilled over. "Because I wondered the same thing for many years. I figured for my mother to leave me, I had to have done something terribly wrong. My father left, my mother left . . . how could I possibly think I was all right? And because I thought something was wrong with me, I didn't make friends, either. I was afraid to

risk becoming attached . . . afraid of loving. I bet that's
why Ryan isn't making friends."

"But he's attached to me and you."

"You're the constant in his life. And like you said
before, I was more like Santa Claus. But this time I
stayed longer, and he got attached. Sometimes we can't
help getting connected even though we're trying to protect ourselves from it."

Max's hands clenched at his sides, but his voice was
even. "It sounds as if he's been thinking about all this
quite a bit. That could be why he's distracted at school.
I'll talk to Mrs. Barrett so she knows what's going on."

Pounding feet down the stairs brought Tessa to her
feet. Ryan hopped down the last one and held out his
hand to Tessa. It was his favorite car, a red Ferrari.
"You take this along so you don't forget about us."

Tessa realized Ryan still needed reassurance, and
probably the best thing she could do was to leave and
then return as she said she would so he'd understand he
could trust her. She took the car and put it in her purse.
"I'll take very good care of it." Leaning down, she
kissed him on the cheek and gave him a final hug.

She didn't like leaving . . . she didn't like it at all.

Away from the fires, bustle and confusion Friday
evening, Tessa picked up the phone in her hotel room.
She'd managed a call to Max and Ryan from a fire station Wednesday evening. Turning Ryan's small car over
in her hand, she smiled. When she'd called the night
she'd arrived, he'd still seemed somewhat anxious.
When she'd called Wednesday, he'd jabbered to her for
a good fifteen minutes about school and Scruffy.

Now Max . . . he was another story.

He'd been civil...polite...as if nothing had happened between them in the past six weeks. Didn't he care at all what she was doing? Didn't he care if she came back? He certainly didn't sound as if he did. So much had changed during her stay with him this time. *She* had changed. Because right now she didn't care about the brushfires or her byline. All she cared about was getting back to Max and Ryan. The fires, Dan's photographs, the interviews—none of it generated its usual excitement. She felt like a different person. Even Dan had noted a change and commented on her lack of enthusiasm for a story that would engender publicity and add a distinguished notch to their career belts.

Jabbing in Max's phone number, Tessa waited expectantly for him to answer.

But an eight-year-old voice piped up, "Is that you, Tessa?"

Her thumb rimmed the hood of Ryan's toy car. "Hi, pancake. What's cooking?"

He giggled and launched into a description of the clubhouse Jimmy's dad was building for him. When he was finished, he asked tentatively, "When are you comin' home?"

"Home" was taking on new meaning for her. "Tomorrow."

As if satisfied, he asked, "You wanna talk to Dad now?"

"You bet." She heard Ryan say to Max, "She's comin' home tomorrow."

Max's voice had little intonation. "Your work is finished?"

"Yes."

"You and Holloway coming back together?"

"No. Dan's staying a few days."

"Where are you now?"

"In a hotel in L.A."

"Holloway with you?"

"He's in the same hotel." Could Max be jealous? The idea made her smile ... and hope. "Are you going to compete with Jimmy's dad?" she asked softly, wanting to get back to an easy relationship with Max.

"A clubhouse? Ryan and I talked about it. But I think a jungle gym might be more beneficial. Come spring, we'll see."

Come spring. The phrase hung between them. "Will you be home tomorrow when I get back? My flight will get in about eleven. I'll be there early afternoon."

"We don't have any plans. I'm sure Ryan will want to stay home and wait for you."

And what about you? she asked silently. Taking a risk, a giant step forward with her heart pounding, she admitted, "I've missed you and Ryan."

Silence met her until Max said in a gruff voice, "You had a call from a Jason Vandemeer."

Vandemeer was an important name in newspaper publishing. It was rumored that he was going to start up a news publication. "Did he say what he wanted?"

"No, just that it was important he reach you. Here's his number." Tessa copied it on the notepad beside the phone. It was the same area code as the Jenkins–New Haven region.

"Anything else?" she asked, just wanting to get Max to talk to her.

"No. I'll see you tomorrow. Ryan wants to say goodbye."

She spent a few more minutes talking to Ryan, then hung up, her heart sinking. She wanted to tell Max she loved him so badly, but she wasn't sure he wanted to hear it. And she didn't know if she could risk another rejection in her life.

The tension between Max and Tessa was a palpable fog. She'd been back for three days and they'd all been the same. If she got too close, he backed away. She stepped into a room; he left it. Except when Ryan was around, he treated her like a pariah, or worse yet, a stranger. The only productive conversation they'd had alone concerned Max's conference with Mrs. Barrett. She'd agreed with Tessa that they'd probably discovered the root of Ryan's problem. Now that it was out in the open, they could all give him the reassurance he needed.

By Monday morning, Tessa was angry, hurt and overwhelmed by a love for Max that was as confusing as his actions. She'd tried to phone Jason Vandemeer all weekend, but had only reached his answering machine. Finally, Monday morning, the man himself answered. Preferring not to discuss his business with her on the phone, he asked her to meet with him at his office in New Haven that afternoon.

Thankful for the distraction, Tessa waited in a reception area of a plush office building. She'd be leaving for the Summit on Saturday and didn't know what to do about Max. Did he expect her to leave and not come back for a few months? Did he want her to spend Thanksgiving with him? Christmas? If he didn't love her, she didn't want to force her presence on him. If he did love her, wouldn't he ask her to stay? And what would she say? I'll give up my career for you and Ryan? Could she do that?

"Ms. Kahill?"

She looked up to find an older gentleman, gray-haired, spectacled and distinguished-looking, motioning for her to come into his office. His eyes skimmed up her black tailored slacks and white oxford shirt. When she reached the doorway, he extended his hand. "I'm Jason Vandemeer."

Tessa nodded and shook his hand. "It's a pleasure to meet you."

He let her precede him into the office and instead of taking the chair behind his desk, he sat in one of the two in front of it as did she. "Are you curious why I asked to see you?"

"Intrigued, actually. Is it true you're starting your own publication?"

When he grimaced, his glasses slipped down his nose a little. He shoved them up. "No secrets in this business, are there?"

She smiled. "You want to keep it a secret?"

"Until I got the right backing, I did. But we're ready to roll now. A press release went out today."

"Do you want me to free-lance for you?" she asked eagerly, knowing his valued reputation in publishing, his track record of success with the newspapers he'd owned.

"No. I want you to be my news editor."

The offer hit her like a streak of lightning. "You're kidding!"

"I couldn't be more serious, Ms. Kahill. May I call you Tessa?"

She nodded, stunned beyond words.

"I know you're still young, but that's nothing a few years won't fix. Truthfully, all I'm interested in is your experience, and you have plenty of that. You've worked with editors, other journalists, photographers. You know quality work better than I do.''

''You're sure?''

His blue eyes knowingly met hers, and she realized he assessed character as thoroughly as he did journalistic expertise. ''I've been aware of your work for some time. Then I saw your interview on WHBT and suspected you were exactly what I needed. Since then, I've talked with your editors, your colleagues, and now I'm sure. The question is, can you give up one kind of excitement for another? You'd be stuck in New Haven most of the time, but I think the challenge of putting the magazine together would more than make up for it.''

''You'll be *here*? Not in New York?''

''There are advantages, manageable expenses being the major one. With fax machines and conference calls, New Haven is perfect.''

''News editor,'' she said more to herself than to him.

''I know you're covering the Summit. I'd like your answer when you get back.'' He gave her a sly smile. ''I don't suppose you could give me your decision to-day?''

She shook her head, mentally listing the pros and cons, thinking about Max and Ryan. ''This would be a big change. I wouldn't have time to free-lance.''

''Maybe when you're on vacation,'' he teased.

What would Max think if she took the job in New Haven? Would he realize she needed to be close to him and Ryan? Would he accept the career move as a compromise? Would he understand she wanted to stay here and love him?

Tessa had planned to talk to Max about the job offer, but after they put Ryan to bed and she stopped in her room to run a brush through her hair, he'd disappeared. He'd honed his avoidance skills to an art form.

She hurried through the first floor, her palms sweaty. This conversation could be the most important one of her life. Going down the hallway to his bedroom, she saw his door standing open. When she peeked inside, she felt she was trespassing. Black socks lay in balls beside the bed; his jeans tilted over the side. One of the drawers in his dresser wasn't quite closed. The king-size bed drew her eye over and over.

Pulling herself away, she went to the kitchen. Where could he be?

Listening to the house's silence for a hint, she heard a thump-thump she thought she recognized. She went to the door and opened it. The garage light cast its glow on the driveway. Max pounded the basketball against the pavement over and over.

Closing the door behind her, she crossed to the driveway. The November chill nipped at her and she crossed her arms, rubbing above her elbows. Max didn't hear her or see her as she approached.

He was amazing to watch. The white T-shirt was damp with perspiration and molded to his shoulders, showing the play and purpose of every push on the ball. His gray jogging pants rode low on his hips, the white string dangling from the waistband.

Abruptly he stopped dribbling, pivoted and shot for the basket. The ball hit the backboard, circled the rim and fell into the net. Max caught it, slapping it against the macadam in the same driving rhythm as before.

Tessa didn't know how long she stood watching, fascinated by this man she loved.

Max couldn't work off the worry that had coalesced into an avalanche of anger, concern and jealousy as each day had passed with Tessa in California. What was she doing? Was she in danger? Was Dan Holloway holding her in his arms? And when she came back, she'd acted as if she hadn't been away, with her smiles and her damn green eyes inviting him to talk to her, be friends, forget she'd be leaving again in a few days, this time for a long time. She had a life. She'd taken time out of it for him and Ryan. So why in the hell couldn't he be grateful?

Because damn it to blazes, he didn't want her to leave! He slammed the basketball against the garage door with every ounce of strength he possessed and watched it bounce crazily toward the house.

Then he saw her. With her arms wrapped around her, protecting herself from the cold. He didn't feel cold. He'd only felt heat since Tessa had returned. A burning, consuming heat that defied who he was and who she was and a life they couldn't share.

He knew he looked like hell. He was sweaty, breeze-blown and disheveled. Tucking his T-shirt more securely into his jogging pants, he muttered, "What are you doing out here?"

"Looking for you." Her gaze attached to his hand as it slid from the back of his waist to the front.

Feeling his body respond to her hungry stare, he answered gruffly, "You've found me. What do you need?" He couldn't tell in the play of shadows and light, but he thought he saw her blush.

"I wanted to talk to you. But that can wait. What about a little one-on-one?"

Damn, if she didn't usually take him by surprise. "You think you have a chance?"

"There's no harm in trying. I can use the workout."

"You might want to get your sweatshirt—"

Scooping up the ball, she bounced it in front of her. "I'm fine. Let's play."

He was amazed at her speed if not her finesse. And she was sneaky. Slipping under his arm, sidestepping and managing a shot he never expected her to make. She couldn't guard him, though. All he had to do was reach over her, around her. Trouble was he could smell her, feel her, touch her, and she was driving him crazy with her hair tousled, loose curls bobbing around her face, her breasts lifting her sweater each time she breathed, her tongue snaking over her lips as she concentrated on defending her territory.

Eyes on the ball, she danced in front of him, her arms ready to reach, lower or grab.

He thought he was quick enough. He thought he could outmaneuver her. After all, he was a lot bigger, a lot stronger and a lot more experienced. He jumped. She blocked. The ball sailed high and off kilter. Her cheek met his chest, his arms went around her, their feet tangled and they fell against the garage door. His shoulder hit the wood, but he held Tessa to him to protect her as much as he could.

Once they were steady, he felt her take a deep breath and wondered if he was crushing her. Loosening his grip, he lowered his chin. Tessa's hold on him didn't ease. But she raised her head and the longing in her beautiful green eyes burned into his soul. Coherent thought, logic, reality, swirled around in his head as passion exploded. His lips sealed to hers, branding her, claiming her, possessing her.

Plunging into her mouth, his tongue swept against hers with a ferocious intensity he couldn't restrain. She responded by stroking and tasting him, digging her fingers into his back and pressing against him. Inflamed beyond caution and control, he slipped his hand under the hem of her sweater to touch her softness and assuage his need.

When she arched into his palm, he hastily pulled up her bra and finally felt her in his hand. She was everything he imagined; everything he could want or need. His finger sought and found her nipple—peaked, hardened, ready for him. Brushing his finger back and forth, back and forth, she moaned into his mouth and slid her hands down his back into the waistband of his pants. She pulled out his T-shirt, and when he felt her fingers on his backside, he separated her legs with his knee.

He broke off the kiss and took a detour down her neck so he could hear her as well as taste her. Each small, erotic sound took him to a new height of arousal until Tessa was all he heard, thought or felt. Pushing her sweater and bra out of his way, he bent to her breast.

As his lips closed around her, she cried out. And when the tip of his tongue probed her, she murmured, "I love you, Max."

This was a Tessa he didn't know, one he'd only dreamed about. Responsive, loving, free.

Free?

The cold night air wound around him as a more penetrating cold invaded his heart. She wasn't free. She was married to a job that took her from country to country, through fires and wars and floods. His love could never replace the excitement of her work. His love and Ryan's would only tie her down. She'd resent him, she'd resent them, and he'd lose her just as he'd lost her nine years ago.

Tessa had never intended to say those three words just now, just this way. But the emotion had escalated and overflowed from her heart, until the words were as natural as Max's kiss, his touch, her body's ready response. Had he heard her? Had he realized she'd taken the biggest risk of her entire life?

When his mouth left her breast and he straightened, she thought he was going to respond. She thought she was finally going to learn how he felt—

He stepped back as if she were the last woman on earth he wanted to touch. The expression on his face was so stony, she wondered where the passionate man who'd been creating a fire storm inside her had gone. "Max?"

"What are we doing to each other, Tessa? Five days and you'll be gone. Why do you think I've been avoiding you? So this kind of thing wouldn't happen."

She reached out to touch his arm.

He stepped back. "Don't play with fire. I'm at my limit, Tessa. Go into the house before I forget I'm a gentleman and I take advantage of a miserable situation." When she didn't move, he said more loudly, "Go on. Find something else to do to make the time pass before you're off on your next assignment."

His words hurt as much as his rejection. She'd given him her heart, and he didn't want it. He wanted her gone. She was a temptation...a miserable situation. How often she'd felt like that in the past. In the orphanage, in the foster homes, in school. If Max loved her, he'd accept her the way she was. He'd accept her career and be willing to work on some sort of compromise. She'd said she loved him, and he didn't care.

So why would he care if she told him about the job in New Haven? She could never be what he wanted. And she'd learned long ago, if she wasn't herself, she was nobody at all. He wanted her to leave him alone, so she'd do just that.

Fighting tears that would serve absolutely no purpose, she straightened her sweater, squared her shoulders, avoided Max's gaze and marched into the house, wishing it were her home, wishing Max and Ryan were her life.

Chapter Ten

Silence surrounded Max as he stepped into the kitchen Thursday afternoon and closed the back door. The quiet seemed unnatural. Usually, he heard Ryan playing or chattering, Tessa rattling pots and pans or talking on the phone. Then he remembered. Last night Tessa had said she'd pick up Ryan at school today and take him shopping for new sneakers and jeans. He was outgrowing everything.

The past week had been pure torture for Max, seeing Tessa, living with her, avoiding her because it hurt too much to love her and not ask her to stay. He couldn't ask this time. It had to be her choice, a free choice. No pressure. No coercion.

Tugging down his tie, Max went to the living room and picked up the mail lying by the phone. The light blinked on the answering machine. He automatically pushed the button.

"Tessa, Vandemeer here. Just a reminder that I need your decision about the job with *You and the News* as soon as possible, though I'll wait until after the Summit if I have to. There's something else I'd like to talk to you about. I'll be here tonight. Give me a call."

The tape clicked and rewound.

You and the News. Max had read about it in the paper recently and recognized Vandemeer's name from the phone call he'd taken for Tessa while she was away. He'd figured the magazine wanted her to do an article. But apparently Vandemeer had offered Tessa a job. A permanent position? Why hadn't she said something?

Max slapped the bills in his hand back down on the end table. The answer was simple. Tessa wasn't going to take it. A job, in one place, for any length of time? Not Tessa.

Max had heard Tessa's murmured "I love you" when they'd almost made love in the driveway. And as he suspected, it had been uttered in the throes of passion. That kind of love wasn't enough. He'd been right to pull back. Just two more days to go, and she'd be gone. The emptiness in his heart rivaled the emptiness in his soul.

While Ryan rushed to find Max, Tessa took off her coat and found a scrap of paper on the kitchen counter with the scrawled message, "Call Vandemeer. He'll be there until late tonight."

Did Max know about the job offer? Had Vandemeer himself talked to Max or had he left a message? If Max knew...

She dialed Vandemeer's number so she'd know where she stood before she approached Max.

"Vandemeer here."

"Mr. Vandemeer, it's Tessa Kahill. I received a message that you called."

"I should have just told you on the machine. I have a packet of material you might want to read before you make your decision. You can pick it up any time. I've included a list of names I'm considering to head the different departments as well as editorial staff. I'd like your feedback."

She twisted the phone cord around her finger. "But what if I decide not to take the job?"

"I'd still like your input. Is that a problem?"

"No, I suppose not. I have to run a few errands tomorrow. I'll pick it up then."

"That's fine. Tessa, I'll admit to an ulterior motive here. The more interested and involved you become, the more I'm hoping you'll be convinced this job is the right career move for you."

"I appreciate your candor. I'll see you tomorrow."

Tessa hung up the phone. As she'd suspected, Vandemeer had left a message on the machine. Max hadn't spoken with the publisher so he didn't know about the offer. If she told him now...

Maybe he'd realize she was willing to change the direction of her career. Maybe it would make a difference.

Following the sound of Ryan's voice, Tessa went to Max's bedroom. She found Ryan settled next to his dad on the bed, still wearing his coat. His head was bowed as Max gestured to something across his knees. Standing in the doorway, Tessa could see it was a photo album.

Max pointed to a picture. "And that's your mother baking your first birthday cake."

Ryan hunched over the pictures as if by getting very close, he'd remember Leslie better. Tessa backed into the hall, upset, hurting, afraid to interrupt the private moments between father and son. Apparently Max had been hovering over the album when Ryan went in.

Max was still grieving. He still loved Leslie more than he could love a woman in his present. That's why he couldn't ask her to stay. He was still too wrapped up in the past. She didn't mean enough to Max for him to ask her to spend her life with him.

Maybe this was a payback for her leaving him nine years ago. Maybe this was a sign that her fragile dream of roots and a home would never come to be. The pain welling up inside her was much too familiar. But this time, unlike so many before, she let the tears fall and climbed the steps to the guest room to get her notes together for the Summit. That was all she had left.

Saturday morning the suitcase sat open on Tessa's bed. It wasn't as though she had a lot to pack. Folding a sweatshirt, she laid it in neatly.

A small rap sounded on the door.

"Come in."

Ryan pushed the door, and it swung open with a creak. He looked as if she were going away forever, with his long face and sad eyes. She wished she could change things for both of them.

Crossing to the bed, he held out his red Ferrari. "I want you to take it with you so you don't forget me."

She'd returned the car to him after her trip to California. "I'll never forget you, pancake. But I'll take it if you want me to." He nodded, and she wished she could pack him in her suitcase and take him with her.

"You're not gonna live here anymore, are you?"

"No. But I promise I'll come back and visit as I always have."

His expression told her that wasn't much comfort. Maybe he needed something tangible to hold onto, too. She pulled her chain out from under her sweater—the chain she hadn't removed since Max had clasped it around her neck. Holding the ring, she slid the chain through it, put it on her pinkie and reattached the chain.

Sure she was doing the right thing, she crooked her finger at Ryan and perched on the bed. He came over with questions in his brown eyes that were the same dark shade as his father's. Taking his hand, she opened his small fingers and set the circle of gold in his palm. "This was my mother's. It's the only thing I have of hers and it's very important to me. I want you to keep it someplace safe so you'll know I will be back. I won't forget about you. And if ever you and your dad need me..." That had just slipped out, but she meant it. "All you have to do is call."

"Across the ocean?"

"If it's very important, you can call across the ocean."

Ryan threw his arms around her, the ring closed tightly in his hand. "I love you, Tessa."

"I love you, too, honey." She blinked back tears, not wanting Ryan to see how upset she was. By tomorrow at this time, she'd be on a plane to Norway and Max's and Ryan's lives would get back to normal. That would be best for Ryan.

Remembering that the next afternoon, she said her final goodbye to the eight-year-old whom she'd come to love so deeply. He stood in the kitchen looking out the window as Max carried her suitcase and computer to the car. Always the gentleman.

As she stood at the edge of the driveway with Max after he'd set her luggage in the trunk and closed it, she felt she had to take one final stab at a chance for a future with him. "Do you want me to come back for Thanksgiving?"

Something hot and dark and hungry flickered in his eyes for the briefest moment. Then it was gone. "That's up to you."

So much for that last chance. "I'll let you know," she murmured. Thinking about whether she should or shouldn't consider it hurt too much right now.

Walking away from Max was the hardest thing she'd ever done. But she did it. She opened the door to the driver's side. "Take care of yourself, Max. And Ryan." She didn't wait for his response. She couldn't or her tears would blind her.

The Monday before Thanksgiving, Max went into Ryan's room to put his son's clean clothes away. Ryan was sitting on the floor by his bed, a shoe box between his legs. Max knew his son kept his treasures in that box—a six-inch-long feather he'd found in the park, rocks of all shapes and sizes that had grabbed his attention for one reason or another, a few baseball cards, a cat's-eye marble that had belonged to Max. But in his hand now, something gold and round glittered.

Max shoved Ryan's socks into a drawer. "What is that, slugger?"

Ryan closed his hand around the object, reminding Max of Tessa's protective gesture when ... Max walked over to Ryan slowly. Tessa had been on his mind even when he was teaching. She'd been gone over a week. He couldn't sleep. He didn't care if he ate. If it weren't for Ryan ...

He sat on the floor beside his son. "Can I see it?"

Ryan opened his hand. "Tessa gave it to me."

Max's heart raced. "When?"

"Before she left."

Max gently rubbed his thumb over a fiery opal. "It's very special to her."

"She told me it was her mommy's. She gave it to me so I know she'll be back."

"But maybe not very soon," Max murmured.

"Dad, did you ask Tessa to stay?"

A sharp pain stabbed Max's heart. "She couldn't stay, Ryan. She has a job to do." He'd watched the reporters on the news last evening in Oslo, scurrying around diplomats, trying to get the first word on negotiations.

"But did you *ask* her?" Ryan pressed insistently.

Max turned the ring over in his hand. "No, I didn't."

"But, Dad, she'd stay if you'd ask her. She'd live with us. I *know* she would."

"Ryan..."

"She said if you or me need her, she'll come. She said it. And we need her, don't we?"

Was it as simple as Ryan made it sound? If he had asked Tessa to stay, would she have stayed?

"Don't we, Dad?"

With increasing clarity, Max realized his son was right. They did need her. "Yes, we do."

"She said if it was really important, we could call her 'cross the ocean. Honest." Ryan made a cross over his heart.

"I believe you. But I have a lot of things to think about first. Do you mind if I hold on to Tessa's ring for tonight? I promise I'll be very careful with it, and I'll give it back to you tomorrow."

"Will it help you think?"

"It might."

Hours later, Max stared at the circle of gold as the bedside lamp made it glow. The turmoil he'd felt earlier had been nothing compared to now. He loved Tessa.

He loved her so much, every part of him ached for her. And he'd let her walk out of his life. He'd been a damn fool.

He'd been so caught up in his own wants and needs, he hadn't seen hers. With a childhood like Tessa's, she needed reassurance; she needed a hand held out to her. Before she could commit herself, she needed the sure knowledge that he loved her. He mentally kicked himself again for being so self-absorbed that he'd been deaf and blind to all the signs.

She'd proven her love over and over again every day she'd been with them. He could see her love for Ryan so clearly. But he'd been afraid to see it for himself. She had even *said* she loved him. Dismissing it as passion talking, he'd ignored it. Tessa never said anything she didn't mean. But he'd been afraid to hear it probably as much as she'd been afraid to say it. Because he feared it wasn't enough. Because he was afraid she'd leave him again as she had nine years ago.

Tessa was afraid of being abandoned, being rejected yet another time. So was he. Because of her leaving before, because of Leslie's death, he, too, was afraid of being abandoned. He just hadn't wanted to admit it. As he'd studied the pictures in the photo album, he'd realized he'd looked on Leslie's death as a betrayal. He'd been angry at Tessa for leaving; he'd been angry with Leslie for leaving.

But now it was time to let go of the anger and move on. His actions the past couple of weeks probably had convinced Tessa he *didn't* love her. Max swore violently, disgusted with himself. So now what could he do?

Only one thing gave him hope. Her question before she left. *Do you want me to come back for Thanksgiving?* Lord, yes, he did. And maybe if he told her he loved her, she'd reconsider taking the job in New Haven, or another one in New York, or one anywhere else in the same country so they could share a life. She mattered too much to let her get away a second time. He'd made her career an insurmountable stumbling block. But it didn't have to be one. They could work something out.

Flexibility had never been his strong suit, but somehow he'd adjust. To be with Tessa, he'd do almost anything.

Max checked his bedside clock. It was probably around 5:00 a.m. in Oslo. The Summit wouldn't be over for another day. If he called now...

Before he lost his nerve, he found the number that Tessa had given him and dialed. The hotel rang her room, and he held his breath.

"Hello?" She sounded sleepy.

"Tessa? It's Max."

"Max! What's wrong? Has something happened to Ryan?"

"No," he was quick to reassure her. "Ryan's fine."

He heard her sigh of relief. "Then I don't understand...."

He turned the ring around on the tip of his thumb. "I wanted to know if you've made plans for after the Summit."

Her hesitation tortured him as he prayed she hadn't. Clearing the morning huskiness from her voice, she answered, "Not exactly."

What the hell did that mean? He had visions of her and Holloway or some other journalist who realized how special Tessa was skiing down a mountain.

She went on, "Yesterday I extended my reservations here for a few days. I was going to do some research."

Now was the time to put his heart on the line. As it pounded so loudly he was sure she could hear, he asked, "Will you come back and spend Thanksgiving with us?"

The dead silence almost killed his hope until she asked, "Do you want me to come back for Ryan?"

He laid his heart in her hands. "I want you to come home for me." When she didn't respond, he said, "Tessa?"

Her voice was husky, but he could hear her clearly. "I heard you, Max. I can be there Thanksgiving Day."

Holding herself in check so she didn't break all the speed limits, Tessa pulled up in front of Max's house, not bothering to turn into the driveway after what seemed to be an endless trip. Since Max's call, she hadn't been able to think straight, let alone work efficiently. She'd wanted to drop everything she was doing and fly back immediately. But history and caution made her finish her assignment in Oslo before rushing into...

She wasn't sure what yet. But she was hoping. She was filled with more hope than she ever thought she could hold.

The late-afternoon sun was descending behind tall maples as she pulled her suitcase from the back seat and practically ran to Max's front door. He opened it before she put her hand on the knob. The longing on his face, the desire in his deep brown eyes, his uncertain smile, turned every bone in her body to wobbling sticks.

Dropping her suitcase, she said softly, "I'm home."

Max swept her into his arms and kissed her long and hard with a breathtaking intensity that brought tears to her eyes. Kicking the door shut with his foot, he carried her into the living room and finally put her down in front of the fireplace. It was lit, filling the room with its coziness and warmth. But it was Max's gaze and the caress of his fingers on her cheeks that warmed her inside and out.

"I love you, Tessa. I didn't want to say it for the first time over the phone. I should have said it long before now. But if you'll let me, I'll say it and show you how much I mean it for the rest of our lives."

His words shook her so terrifically, she could hardly stand. Holding onto his broad shoulders, she murmured, "I love you, too. But, Max, I can never take Leslie's place. I'm different. I'm..."

"You're *you*. The woman I love. I don't want you to take Leslie's place. I'll keep her memory alive for Ryan. But it's time for me to let go of the past. I love you for who you are—for all the excitement you bring to my life, for your loyalty, for your passionate caring. I love *you*, sweetheart. And I'm sorry I put us both through hell the past couple of weeks. I guess I was too afraid to risk saying what I felt out loud."

"Max, about my job..."

"We can work something out. I know you can't give up your career. I don't expect you to. But—"

She laid her fingers over his lips. "I was offered a job with a newsmagazine in New Haven."

He didn't seem surprised, but she was when he nibbled at her finger, then said, "I know."

"But how—?"

"When I took the last message from Vandemeer. He mentioned it. I thought you didn't tell me because you weren't considering it and didn't want to stay."

She lovingly stroked his jaw. "I didn't tell you because I didn't know how you felt. I didn't know if you wanted me to stay...."

He lifted her chin and gave her a thorough, deep kiss that she knew would keep their heartfire burning forever. She had no more doubts about his love or where she fit into his life.

When the intensity became almost too much to bear, he tore his mouth from hers and held her tight. After a few moments of their hearts beating in unison, he leaned back. "Do you want to take the job in New Haven?"

"Yes. I'm not afraid to settle down anymore, Max. I'm not afraid to belong. Not if I can be with you."

"I guess I haven't asked the most important question. Will you marry me?"

Tears welled up and her throat tightened, but nothing could prevent her from answering. "Yes, I'll marry you."

The back door slammed shut, and Ryan came running into the living room. "Is the turkey done yet?" Then he saw her. "Tessa!"

He swooped toward her, and Tessa caught him in her arms. Lowering herself to the hearth, she cuddled Ryan against her.

"Did you call her, Dad?" Ryan wanted to know.

Max nodded, not taking his eyes from Tessa's.

"I knew she'd come. Can you stay a long time again?"

"How about if I stay always. If I don't ever leave again?"

"Not ever?"

Max responded, "She might have to make a trip now and then. But she'll always come back to us."

"Like California?"

Tessa answered, "Like California."

The whole thing seemed to be settled for Ryan. "Are we gonna eat soon?"

Max laughed. "It won't be too long. We are missing one thing, though. Dessert. The bakery sold out of pumpkin pies before I got there."

Tessa looked over her shoulder at the beautiful fire leaping and dancing with the warmth and love that filled her heart. "What about toasted marshmallows for dessert? We can make them our tradition."

Max sat on the hearth beside her, curving his arm around her shoulders. "I can't think of a better dessert or a better tradition."

With Ryan on her lap, Max's strong arm around her, Tessa knew she finally belonged. And when Max softly kissed her lips, she was happier than she'd ever been in her life.

Belonging came from loving and being loved. She'd searched the world but had found her heart and her place because of one man, one boy. This Thanksgiving, she knew the true meaning of gratitude. When tears threatened to overflow, she said, "Let's go peek at the turkey and find the marshmallows. We have a Thanksgiving to celebrate."

Ryan's enthusiastic "yeah!" and Max's gentle smile guaranteed this would be a Thanksgiving to remember for always.

Epilogue

On a windy day in late December—after the excitement, rush and joy of Christmas—the hard rap on Tessa's office door brought her head up from the pasteups on her desk.

"Ready for lunch?"

Tessa's stomach fluttered and her heart smiled as Max stepped into her office. It was his Christmas vacation, and they had a date for lunch while Ryan spent the day with a friend. The past two years as Max's wife and Ryan's mother had given Tessa such peace, contentment and fulfillment, she still couldn't believe how happy she was. And now, to be expecting a child, her child and Max's... She still felt grateful and fortunate and, oh, so blessed. Max's parents were going to come for a visit after the baby was born. Max's mother had become a special friend to Tessa, although their relationship was mostly long-distance, just like her relationship with Leslie's mother. Both older women had been a support during this pregnancy.

Tessa stood and pushed back her chair. Max came to her and circled her with his arms. That was a major undertaking these days with her stomach sticking out in front of her.

But Max just rubbed against her gently. "How's he doing?"

She'd had two ultrasounds with Max by her side, holding her hand. On the second one, they could tell the sex of the baby. "He's doing fine. But I can't wait until he makes his appearance so I can see my feet again."

Max smiled indulgently. "Three more weeks. Then the real fun starts—changing diapers, feedings at all hours."

Tessa chucked him on the chin. "You wanted this baby as much as I did. You can't renege now."

"I wouldn't want to."

She sighed. "I worry sometimes."

He twirled one of her curls around his finger. "About?"

"If I can be a good mother."

Max responded immediately. "Just ask Ryan. You're the world's best mother to him. And I second the title."

About six months after she and Max were married, Ryan asked if he could call her "Mom." She'd been so pleased. Remembering her own childhood, she wanted to do everything right. Sometimes she did; sometimes she didn't. And that's why she'd made a decision. If Max agreed. "I talked to Jason today."

"Don't you talk to him every day?" Max teased with a straight face but amusement flickering in his eyes.

"Max, be serious."

He pretended to wipe the smile from his face. "Okay, I'm serious."

She took a deep breath and let it out. "I'm going to take a year's leave of absence."

His black brows arched. "A year? I thought you'd decided on six months."

"I've been thinking. I only have one opportunity to be a mother to this baby. I don't want to miss anything. I'd like a year to be a full-time mother to both this baby and Ryan, maybe more. Before we know it, Ryan will be dating and driving and going to college."

Max's lips twitched. "He's only ten, Tessa."

"But look how fast the past two years have gone!"

Max's gaze took a slow, quiet tour of her face. "You're sure this is what you want?"

"I'm sure, if we can swing it. Jason said if I don't want to come back to a full-time position, he can use me part-time. And if I get bored, I'm supposed to call him and he'll let me free-lance for him. What do you think?"

Max stroked her cheek with his thumb. "I think I'd love to come home to you and our two children every day. But at any time, the rules can change, sweetheart. We've all proven we're adaptable."

Sometimes they ate supper at six, sometimes at seven. Sometimes Max cooked, sometimes Tessa cooked, sometimes they called for pizza. In the summer when Tessa had taken business trips, Ryan and Max had gone with her. The three of them had learned to meld and mesh and adjust. "Maybe you can go back to coaching."

Max shrugged. "Maybe. Or maybe I'll decide we need all the free time together we can get. This baby is going to change our lives."

"But not our love," she murmured.

Max threaded his fingers into her hair and tipped her head up. His kiss expressed his deep desire to be her husband, her lover and her friend, not just now, but for always. They'd keep the homefire burning together, and their heartfire would last forever.

* * * * *

HE'S MORE THAN
A MAN, HE'S
ONE OF OUR

Fabulous Fathers

DADDY'S ANGEL
Annette Broadrick

With a ranch and a houseful of kids to care for, single father Bret Bishop had enough on his mind. He didn't have time to ponder the miracle that brought lovely Noelle St. Nichols into his family's life. And Noelle certainly didn't have time to fall in love with Brett. She'd been granted two weeks on earth to help Brett remember the magic of the season. It should have been easy for an angel like Noelle. But the handsome rancher made Noelle feel all too much like a woman....

Share the holidays with Bret and his family in Annette Broadrick's *Daddy's Angel*, available in December.

Fall in love with our **Fabulous Fathers!**

Silhouette
R O M A N C E™

FF1293

**Silhouette Books
is proud to present
our best authors,
their best books…
and the best in
your reading pleasure!**

Throughout 1993, look for exciting
books by these top names in
contemporary romance:

DIANA PALMER—
The Australian in October

FERN MICHAELS—
Sea Gypsy in October

ELIZABETH LOWELL—
Chain Lightning in November

CATHERINE COULTER—
The Aristocrat in December

JOAN HOHL—
Texas Gold in December

LINDA HOWARD—
Tears of the Renegade in January '94

When it comes to passion,
we wrote the book.

BOBT3

UNDER THE MISTLETOE

*Where's the best place to find love
this holiday season?* UNDER THE MISTLETOE,
*of course! In this special collection, some of
your favorite authors celebrate the joy of the
season and the thrill of romance.*

#976 DADDY'S ANGEL by Annette Broadrick
#977 ANNIE AND THE WISE MEN by Lindsay Longford
#978 THE LITTLEST MATCHMAKER by Carla Cassidy
#979 CHRISTMAS WISHES by Moyra Tarling
#980 A PRECIOUS GIFT by Jayne Addison
#981 ROMANTICS ANONYMOUS by Lauryn Chandler

Available in December from

Silhouette
ROMANCE™

THIS SIDE OF HEAVEN

The miracle of love is waiting to be discovered in Duncan, Oklahoma! Arlene James takes you there in her trilogy, THIS SIDE OF HEAVEN. Look for Book Three in November:

A WIFE WORTH WAITING FOR

Bolton Charles was too close for comfort. Clarice Revere was certainly grateful for the friendship he shared with her son. And she couldn't deny the man was attractive. But Clarice wasn't ready to trade her newfound freedom for love. Not yet. Maybe never. Bolton's patience was as limitless as his love— but could any man wait forever?

Available in November,
only from

Silhouette
R O M A N C E™

If you've been looking for something a little bit different and a little bit spooky, let Silhouette Books take you on a journey to the dark side of love with

Every month, Silhouette brings you two romantic, spine-tingling Shadows novels, written by some of your favorite authors, such as Heather Graham Pozzessere, Anne Stuart, Helen R. Myers and Rachel Lee—to name just a few.

In October, look for:

THE HAUNTING OF BRIER ROSE
by Patricia Simpson
TWILIGHT PHANTASIES
by Maggie Shayne

In November, look for:

TREACHEROUS BEAUTIES
by Cheryl Emerson
DREAM A DEADLY DREAM
by Allie Harrison

In December, look for:

BRIDGE ACROSS FOREVER
by Regan Forest
THE SECRETS OF SEBASTIAN BEAUMONT
by Carrie Peterson

Come into the world of Shadows and prepare to tremble with fear—and passion....
SHAD4